I have heard the mermaids singing

Christopher Bollas

SA 5-24-2012

Published in the United Kingdom 2005
by Free Association Books
57 Warren Street
London W1T 5NR

© 2005 Christopher Bollas

British Library Cataloguing in Publication Data
A catalogue record for this book is available from the
British Library

Produced by Bookchase (UK) Limited
Designed by Pentagram Design Limited
Printed and bound in England

ISBN 1 853437 59 X

I want to thank Robert Timms and Sarah Nettleton for their editorial assistance. I also want to thank my wife, Suzanne, for her comments and support throughout the composition of this work.

Contents

1

Oh, what a lovely depression!

It was 6.19 a.m. and the psychoanalyst, as always, anticipated his 6.20 alarm call by one minute. He had never been sure whether this was an act of unconscious scheduling or whether the clock made an anticipatory click that woke him. But there had been times when, roused by dreams, or his wife's stirrings, or sounds from the night, he had been up before then, listened out for a click, and never heard it; so he tended to believe it was the regularity of his inner clock which woke him on time.

His first patient – today it would be Byron Mourncaster – was not until 9.00 a.m. Before that, he went through his important morning routine, very slowly preparing himself for the day: two cups of tea, toilet and then shower, breakfast of one egg and two slices of fibrous bread. Nowadays he was less interested in his dreams than he had been before because (and he worried about this in his sixties) they really did need more time than he could give them, although now and then a dream could be so deeply wonderful that he recalled it over tea and it followed him about during the day. He had, however, no time at all for nightmares and simply discarded them. After the Catastrophe he had pushed anything troubling out of his mind except for those tribulations brought by his patients, family and friends.

At 8.30 he left his house for the twenty-minute walk to his office. Twice a week he meandered through the park with Westin Moorgate, his journalist friend, but not today. (If asked, the analyst would deny that routine was so important to him; and he did not look the routine-seeking sort, as he was rather unkempt, even dishevelled, and not the sort of character one would associate with a life lived by habit.)

He always looked forward to leaving the house: not until he was outside did he feel that exhilarating separation from the narcissism of being a self – all wrapped up in the mental life and its domestic decisions. Nevertheless, his departures were often tinged with a quite specific anxiety, because on several occasions in the last year he had been stymied by the sight of a neighbour's dog (a most unpleasant-looking creature named Teaser) urinating on the vegetables which were carefully arrayed outside the small market across the street. On this occasion, as every morning, he hoped that his neighbour would already have bought her packet of cigarettes and left, or that the incident would occur – if at all – after he had departed. So he was dismayed to see that less than thirty feet away Teaser was just about to lift his leg on, of all things, the leeks. The analyst crossed the street trying to whisper the word 'no', but instead he produced a croak.

Both grocer and neighbour were struck by this out-of-place sound and stared at him from inside the store. The analyst pointed at the dog and said, 'He's taking a leak.'

The neighbour, Bunnie Hopgood, sprang immediately to her dog's defence.

'What do you mean, he's taking a leek? Don't be absurd.'

'I don't mean he's *taking* a leek, but . . .'

'Of course not,' replied Bunnie, snorting with laughter. 'No dog would be interested in a leek!'

'I meant that your dog was . . .'

'Well, was what then?'

'Was leaking.'

'Leaking? What the hell are you talking about?' Bunnie turned to the shop owner for a second opinion. 'Halis, what do you think he means, "leaking"?'

Halis had only been in the country for two years, and while his command of English may have been less than perfect, he clearly grasped the psychoanalyst's meaning. He ran out from behind the counter to examine his leeks and, sure enough, there was a stream of urine heading south from his vegetable display. 'Oh no,' he said. 'Oh my God.'

'My God what?' asked Bunnie.

'Lady, your dog has pissed on my vegetables.'

'What?'

'Look,' said Halis, pointing at the tell-tale rivulet that had now extended itself five feet along the pavement. 'Look at what your dog has done.'

Bunnie Hopgood ran out of the shop, looked at the leeks, stared briefly at the analyst (who by now was looking at his watch) and positioned her body squarely in front of Halis. 'Are you telling me that Teaser has pissed on your veg? Is that what you're telling me?'

'Look, lady,' explained Halis. 'Seeing is believing. Look, it is dog piss, it is coming out of my leeks.'

'Oh, so you saw him do it, did you? You saw it? How is that possible, Halis, and by the way, I am not "lady", but Bunnie Hopgood, and this is not a dog, this is my Teaser, so let's not treat one another like shits. I come here every day and there is no way that my Teaser is going to piss on your fucking leeks.'

'How it happen then?'

'Well, ask Mr Smarty Pants over there,' she replied. 'Maybe he couldn't bear the sight of a leek without whipping out his dick and pissing on them. He's one of those, those . . .'

'Freudians,' inserted the analyst.

'Yes, one of those Freudians, so he probably had a Freudian slip, or a Freudian leak. Anyway, what kind of freak runs across the street to report on a dog?' She turned towards the accused. 'Teaser is no fool. He knows a pervert when he sees one. He fucking well knew you were looking at his raised leg and you put him off.'

'Mrs Hopgood, please, for goodness' sake,' pleaded the analyst. 'Let's forget this. I've—'

'Yes, you've got to leave, haven't you? Having created this havoc, having fucked with my Teaser, you think you can just walk off, leaving this trail of piss behind you.'

The analyst was in a real fix; and he blamed himself for it. Why hadn't he just walked on and let the dog piss on the leeks? That was the question. But he quite simply wasn't the sort of person who could do so. In fact, he and Westin had been talking only the previous week about the necessity of ordinary civic action. Westin had told the psychoanalyst how he had walked into a violent domestic dispute on the High Street, in front of Heaven's Buns bakery. A man had just punched a woman on the arm with enough force to knock her to the ground. When Westin stepped in and asked what the man was doing, the guy hit him in the face, dropping him to the pavement, with the reply: 'That's what I'm doing, asshole. What the fuck do you think I'm doing?' Whereupon

4

the woman jumped up, kicked Westin in the leg (he was still on the ground at this point), and shouted: 'You leave my Henry alone!' Westin apparently then struggled to his feet and backed into the doorway of Heaven's Buns, but simultaneously tried to continue the 'conversation':

'I thought "your Henry" was beating you up!' he protested.

'Yeah, and so what if he was? What business is that of yours?' the woman yelled back. (When recounting the story, Westin carefully described the blood vessels pulsating on her rather beautiful soft white neck.)

'Well, I think it's the duty of any citizen to step in when something like that is happening,' Westin reasoned, before the man butted in again:

'Citizen?' the bloke laughed. 'What the fuck is a citizen, you stupid wanker!'

The two of them had then gone off, leaving poor Westin humiliated and confused.

Westin Moorgate and the psychoanalyst spent quite some time reflecting on this episode. They talked about what indeed it did mean to be a citizen, especially in this so-called modern world. Initially they went through the usual societal tics: where were the police when you really needed them? Why couldn't they turn the traffic wardens – who swarmed about the city like locusts – into a kind of neighbourhood Dad's Army to protect people from the ordinary crimes of the day? But they soon got on to the fact that now and then we will all find ourselves alone with the potential for heroic action, or for failure as a citizen. A citizen had to be one who took responsibility for *civitas*, and therefore had an implied licence to intervene in certain circumstances when the law was being broken. It was somewhat in that vein that the analyst had prevailed upon Teaser not to piss on the leeks. As Westin said, it was not a matter of choice, it was a sort of drive: if you are a citizen, you just jump in. This sort of person was almost always referred to as a 'have-a-go hero', someone who simply could not turn away from the sight of criminal activity. Needless to say, Westin Moorgate had not foreseen how his intervention would be construed by the apparent victim; although afterwards he recalled that battered women often defended their attackers, and later the same week he wrote an article on citizenship under the banner 'Leave My Henry Alone'. In the essay he traced the origin of the idea of citizenship and, having outlined some of its properties, he concluded that ambivalence towards the contemporary state had seeped down into a private loathing of being a citizen in the first place. Thus those who acted on behalf of *civitas* were seen as creeps who were upsetting the apple-cart, that cart now being a world composed of state-sanctioned anarchism.

During their next walk the psychoanalyst had suggested to Westin that the Catastrophe had unconsciously ended citizenship because the state could no longer protect its citizens. Even though people genuinely needed more police on the streets and were indeed frightened of terrorists, there was a latent rage against the failure of state structures to deliver on the promise of effective government of any kind, and so people were now developing an anarchic mentality. At the very moment of needing more assurance, since we could no longer rely upon the state to protect us, this failure led to what Anna Freud used to call 'identification with the aggressor'. So when Westin stepped in to act as a citizen, he unwittingly offended everyone. No one thought well of his action. He was out of order.

Indeed, when the police did eventually arrive – only because Westin insisted a report be filed – they had not known what to say to him. While he had perhaps anticipated a pat on the back, Mrs Stottlemeyer (a woman who seemed to inhabit Heaven's Buns and had witnessed the incident in its entirety) said that Westin had, in her view, behaved in a high-handed manner, and that he had intervened in a purely domestic dispute. 'I am quite sure,' she had said, slowly and emphatically, 'that *that woman* had it coming to her.' When the police seemed momentarily taken aback, she had looked with contempt at Westin and concluded: 'Well, our hero was on the ground when *she* kicked him! So he wasn't exactly rescuing Helen of Troy, was he?' The cops' laughter only added to his bewilderment. However, he subsequently wondered in his essay whether the police had gone beyond accepting crime as a way of life – which was not news – and had moved on to a more disturbing vision: that crime *was* life. To live a life of crime was therefore simply to be alive, to live like everyone else.

Some of these thoughts were in the psychoanalyst's mind as he headed to his office that morning, pondering the wisdom of his intervention with Bunnie Hopgood. He knew, however, that soon he would be immersed in Byron Mourncaster's world of depression, and as he picked up his espresso from Hippo, still his café of choice, the thought occurred to him that depression might be a form of political responsibility. Maybe those who were depressed, he mused, were actually holding the state together. Maybe they were the quiet glue in a social fabric that was otherwise headed toward chaos as depression – in a way, protecting people from disorder, as they were too bummed to be anarchic.

Mourncaster had been quite a challenge for the psychoanalyst. This patient embraced his depression with such tenacity that for a long time the analyst was perplexed, until the day when – as was so often the case in his line of work – an idea had popped up without prior consideration.

'Mr Mourncaster, I think your despair is like a partner, and there is room only for the two of you.'

Mourncaster asked what the analyst meant. He replied that whenever he addressed Mourncaster's depression it was as if the analyst were some sort of intruder, interrupting a form of intimacy.

'Why the hell would I want my depression as a partner?' asked Mourncaster.

'Because then you don't have to do anything,' replied the analyst.

'No, I'm depressed and therefore *can't* do anything,' said Mourncaster.

'Yes, it's *your* depression doing this, isn't it?'

'Why do you put it that way?'

'I rather think that's the way *you* put it, don't you?' continued the analyst.

'What, you think I *intentionally* seek out depression so that I then don't have to do anything?'

'Well, it's rather like wearing a "Handicapped" sign so that you can park in the disabled areas of life. As long as you suffer from depression, which you talk of as if it were a thing, or an other, then you are free of all responsibility. Your depression is responsible for you.'

'Well, why would I do something like that?'

'Because up to a point it works.'

In that session and others to follow the analyst gradually pointed out how Mourncaster's depression was a silent partner to whom he was married, and that this of necessity had to exclude any other partner. Mourncaster himself admitted that whenever he met a woman – he was a rather tall, broodingly attractive sort of character – he soon confessed to her that he was depressed; to which the analyst replied that this was like saying he was married. Time passed and gradually Mourncaster's love relation to his depression abated and he could allow for differing sorts of affairs – indeed, on occasion with actual people, and eventually with a woman whom he rather took to.

To be fair to Mourncaster, the post-Freudian world, by which the psychoanalyst meant the world *after* the departure of the unconscious, had silently embraced disturbances of thought, feeling or behaviour by converting everything into a relationship. Byron Mourncaster wasn't the only one telling everyone of his depression: the depressed of the northern hemisphere were competing to get on radio talk shows and discuss how it had infiltrated their lives and ruined their existence. But the same was true of those who were, say, alcoholics. They weren't just overdrinking, they were having a relationship. 'I am an alcoholic', 'I am a compulsive gambler' or 'I am a workaholic' were secular conversion experiences, with people rushing into twelve-step programmes full of other worshippers who had placed their illness before life with others. Chronic fatigue syndrome was as good a description of everyone's ailment as could be found, reckoned the psychoanalyst, as it was a way of putting one's fatigue first. 'Sorry, but I can't hang out with you because I suffer from CFS' was something which the analyst understood as 'Sorry, but I can't hang out with you because there is nothing meaningful in my life any more except the exhaustion suffered from being empty, and I must now put that first.'

So Mourncaster's despair was part of a widespread cultural movement. Indeed, the psychoanalyst was currently encumbered by such an unusually high number of depressed analysands that he was forced to reconsider the whole conundrum posed by the word 'depression'. Earlier that year he had been extensively travelling the backroads of his home country – something he liked to do every few years, as he found shards of childhood memory embedded in objects like telephone poles or dirt roads or abandoned railway lines. As he drove he would listen to the radio, and one day there was a programme on depression. The psychiatrist being interviewed said that depression was an illness, and that thousands of people had it. It was important not to deny this illness, he explained, but to declare that one suffered from it and then to seek help, by which the psychiatrist meant the person was to take one or other of the many available anti-depressants.

This kind of argument infuriated the psychoanalyst because it declared that an area of human experience should be eradicated through psychotropic ingestion. Why not summarise the programme more accurately: 'Are you suffering from being human? Do things get you down? Is life beyond you? Problems with relationships? Trouble with your boss? Then don't deny your problem any longer. Being human is an illness. Get help.' But they don't quite put it that way, do they? They use paranoid language, the analyst noted, to suggest how a self is being taken over: 'Has depression infiltrated your work life and invaded your most intimate relations? Is this silent enemy now threatening your future? If you suffer from this disease, if it's trying to take over your entire life, we at Dawn Chemical have the solution, just as we had in Vietnam. But we have much better control over it now than we did then – after all, progress is very important to us – and so we now recommend that you take Napalmtrek®. The correct dosage of Napalmtrek® can exfoliate the human kinks, leaving you serene and trouble-free.'

Well, they pissed him off, these programmes.

After he recalled hearing the programme on the car radio, the psychoanalyst found himself remembering the first time he had seen Myrna Fallbrook. Tall, in her early thirties, with long black hair and rather cuddly brown eyes, his new patient had plopped into her chair in silence.

The analyst asked why she was there.

'I don't know,' she said.

'You don't know?'

'Well, I guess,' she said, 'I suffer from depression.'

'What depresses you?' he asked.

She said she did not know, but that she was bipolar.

Analysts are meant to listen to their patients with an open mind; but often enough they do go off the rails, and poor Myrna Fallbrook's use of the word 'bipolar' was most unfortunate for her in that moment. The psychoanalyst hated the word more than almost any other. He thought that people who handed the word out should be arrested on the spot. In America nowadays, everybody was 'bipolar' – they had moods, ups and downs, and because to be human in America was now a disease to be eradicated, this diagnosis amounted to a tool of ethnic cleansing.

11

'Who told you you are bipolar?' he asked.

'Oh, some doctors.'

'I see.' The analyst paused. 'Some doctors.'

'Yeah, actually it helped. You see, for a long time I didn't know what the problem was and now I know what I am, so that's a big relief.'

'It's a relief to know that you are bipolar, because now that is what you are?'

'Yeah, now I know there's something wrong with me that I can't do anything about. It's genetic, although they said I should also get some therapy, which is why I decided to come and see you.'

'So, when were you first depressed?'

'I don't know,' she replied, looking at her feet.

'You're looking at your feet.'

'I don't know what to say. Can't you be more directive?'

'You seem irritated by me,' the analyst said.

'No, it's just that I don't see the relevance of your question.'

'About when you were first depressed?'

'Yeah, I don't see how it's relevant.'

And so it went like this for many sessions. She had lost her job – a very prestigious position – and instead of allowing herself to be depressed she had immediately taken another post which turned out to be significantly less challenging. Then, out of the blue, she collapsed and inherited in short order the diagnosis 'bipolar'. The psychoanalyst helped her to understand how her depression was a 'deferred action', how the emotion of losing her job had been denied in the first instance and put off until later, when a second event elicited the suppressed feelings. Fallbrook found it very hard to accept that the comparatively trivial difficulties encountered in her second job could in any way have elicited feelings from the past, but the analyst helped her to see that her current depression was very complex. In the first place, she had unconsciously agreed with Acton – her previous boss – that she was incompetent, and she had carried forth this judgement against herself as a form of intense self-drivenness. When she first faced a small challenge in her new job, some area of her mind told her a cruel part of the world had her in its sights for good.

'But why should I let it get to me like this?' she asked.

'Because a part of you agrees with Acton.'

'Why?'

'Because instead of fighting his judgement at the time, you walked out; and ever since, you've felt that you were cowardly,' said the analyst.

'But I don't see why that would leave me feeling that I can't get up in the morning.'

'Well, why should you get up in the morning if you think it is only to face an Acton?'

'But my current boss is rather nice,' she said, 'nothing like Acton at all.'

'Tell that to your unconscious,' replied the analyst.

He went on to explain that although her present boss was indeed a decent enough person, unfortunately for Fallbrook her unconscious had married Acton – and it was his view of her with which she now agreed, and by which she now assessed herself.

'You are a person with, shall I say, rather merciless demands for perfection,' the analyst said, 'and so when found on this one occasion to be imperfect, you had no option but

13

to agree.'

'I don't know what you're talking about.'

'You don't know what I'm talking about?'

Myrna Fallbrook looked at the floor and went into a deep funk. To say that her brow was furrowed would fail the agricultural metaphor, the analyst thought; it looked more like the trenches from the Great War, and he knew that the battle lines were being drawn before his very eyes.

'It seems to me that you have suddenly declared yourself innocent of a part of your personality,' he said, 'and further that you are rather angry with me for having brought this up.'

His patient remained silent for some five minutes.

He spoke again: 'I think I'm being given the silent treatment.'

'That's because I don't know what you're talking about,' she protested.

'You don't know about a highly demanding part of your personality that judges yourself and others harshly?'

'I don't see what that has to do with anything.'

'So this part of you can, as it were, deem that anything it finds of no significance should just be chucked out on the streets, so to speak.'

At this point Fallbrook startled the analyst. She stared directly at him with a fixed and ferocious look which rather took him aback. After thirty seconds of what he experienced as torture, the following line popped up.

'If looks could kill.'

'What?'

'If looks could kill,' he repeated.

'I don't know what you're talking about.'

The analyst, now nearly recovered, said he thought she was showing him this Acton part of herself. He added that it was like being stared down by an executioner and that it seemed to him to illustrate his point – that she was indeed harbouring a part of her that felt as if it could kill others. As this patient had repeatedly talked of suicide, indeed had constituted an active suicide risk, the analyst then added that he could see why she was afraid she would kill herself.

'And why is that?' she demanded.

'Because you seem to have this kind of love relation with a murderer, and I would have thought that it's very tempting to think of offering yourself up as a kind of sacrificial victim.'

'That's just bullshit,' she said, with a remarkable and exciting venom.

'Well said. I must say, the young innocent girl I saw earlier certainly seems to have left the room. I rather reckon I am left with a terrorist.'

Myrna Fallbrook smiled sarcastically before once again staring at the analyst as if he were an idiot.

'I think I'm meant to be intimidated.'

'Be whatever you want to be,' she said.

'Isn't that an Army slogan?' he asked.

'Anything you want it to be.'

'So you aren't here any more, and I am—'

'Useless,' she interrupted. 'I don't see how this is going to help me at all.'

'Indeed, it would seem we are rather caught up in this cynical part of you that knows how to destroy things, not least all the constructive and helpful aspects of yourself.'

'I don't feel helped by you.'

'Who said I was here to help you?' asked the analyst.
'What?'

'Well, why should I help Joseph Stalin or Adolf Hitler?
Why should I help this part of your personality? Actually, if
some part of you does want to commit suicide, why not lose
the fascist part of yourself?'

Fallbrook's battle-brow now turned more quizzical,
and she seemed genuinely to have understood something.
She sat up from her slouched position.

The psychoanalyst pointed out to her that she seemed
to have changed her frame of mind, to which she said that
she was just in a grouchy mood and was sorry. The analyst
acknowledged that she had reason to feel low, but also said
he thought she was in a funk because she was truly angry
and she had turned the anger inwards. It had originally been
directed at Acton, but she had identified with him and now
was angry with herself. This had worked for a while, he
explained, because one could derive masochistic pleasure
from such self-harm. It was a way of getting a kick out of a
kick; further, it was a way of partly mastering helplessness, as
one actively took part in the attack on the self. In fact, in that
moment, depression was a sort of intermediate mood between
elation ('Aha, you schmuck, you've been caught!') and
dejection ('I'm through for ever'), so if one were engaged in
a kind of self-punitive alliance with one's persecutor then
the depression of apparent worthlessness was somewhat
offset.

That night, at the weekly study group with his colleagues, it
was the psychoanalyst's turn to bring up whatever he wanted

to discuss. He said he thought that depression was actually rather marvellous. He had been working with several depressed patients recently and had decided there was no such thing as 'depression' – instead, there were 'depressions', which he had actually started to classify, as D1, D2, and so on. These various depressions were linked psychodynamically, and he was fascinated to observe the stages and to determine just how many Ds each person had. His colleague Carson Walleye was rather appalled by the analyst's apparent celebration of depression and insisted on an example, so the psychoanalyst talked a bit about Myrna Fallbrook, or 'X', as he referred to her during the group's discussions. He thought he could count up to 25 interconnecting Ds in her overall depression. Carson insisted on a listing, so the analyst slowly and carefully described Fallbrook's depressions as follows:

D1: I am depressed by the fact that 'A' (my boss) thinks poorly of me.

D2: I am depressed by the fact that I agree with him.

D3: I am therefore depressed that I can no longer value myself so highly.

D4: The loss of such self-esteem consequently lowers my self-worth and this is depressing.

D5: Being unfairly struck down by this, I now protest against the injustice by sarcastically saying, 'Well FUCK YOU for making me feel this way and I shall parody your idiocy by being even more of a failure.'

D6: But no one cares when I do this, not even the other parts of my own personality; I feel really quite alone.

D7: I shift my depression by abandoning my context

and deciding to start life anew elsewhere. So I raise hopes, but because I know what this is about, I feel depressed over being less than honest with my new employers.

D8: At the first sign of even the slightest criticism I collapse. I cannot comprehend this and feel I am now truly helpless. I feel no hope, and depression falls upon me like a dark cloud over which I have no control.

D9: Told I am bipolar and given Napalmtrek®, I feel better for a while, but gradually I feel defeated over being classed like this for the rest of my life.

D10: When I try to get up in the morning I have no hope, as I have a disease over which I have no influence. (But this state of hopelessness – my analyst says – is ordinary: who would want to get up and face a Stalinistic part of the self which is just waiting to jump on you for small failures?)

D11: At a loss to do anything myself, dependent on Napalmtrek®, I am now in a vegetative state – because I no longer want to bathe, clothe myself, or eat. My analyst says I am on strike. I am saying, 'Okay, you think I'm fucking up: watch how I bring the whole damn system to a halt.'

D12: My anger over being humiliated by 'A' now joins D11 and my depression is becoming an organised rebellion against my oppression.

D13: My depression now takes the form of doing absolutely nothing. Having continued like this for two months, I am beginning to rather lose it: I am making stupid mistakes, I am forgetting things I would not ordinarily forget, and so on. I find this depression different, as if now there is *truly* something wrong with me.

D14: My depression is now a kind of stupefaction, a *thing* – sort of standing outside me and yet occupying me. I

18

can't think at all. I feel no anger, just nothing.

D15: This brings about inconsolable crying, day after day. I have lost myself.

D16: I ask for help, from anyone I can. Friends come and stay with me. I see my analyst every day, but nothing seems to be any good. I feel I am at the end of my life. The only way out is to kill myself.

D17: The idea of killing myself brings a momentary sense of relief and even triumph, but I do think of everything that I could have been and could have done, and now my sorrow is for a future that I shall not have. My depression is over the loss of my future life and all my children, who will now not be here on this earth with me.

D18: An *overwhelming* question occupies me: how could I have got myself into this situation? To put it another way, how is it that other people get along with things, but I have failed?

D19: My depression now announces itself as my own narrow-mindedness. My analyst welcomes the questioning brought on by D18 and says I have never thought about myself or reflected on my life. I was a kind of machine-woman, just ploughing through one accomplishment after another, not thinking. I feel so low that I cannot think now; indeed, my analyst says he believes I hate thoughts relating to my inner life.

D20: No one in my family thought about their life. We only produced at a high level and if we didn't, we were castigated. Look at my father. Where is this man who promised me so much in my life and who is all shrivelled up and sunk in his own depression? He won't talk and certainly doesn't want to think about anything, except his football team and golf.

D21: I am depressed that I should have to think about all of this when I followed all the rules as a girl and it should have been my father who delivered me into my future. I should not have had to do this for myself, especially as I followed his rules. It's not fair, and I hate the world, and I am depressed that I should be expected to look after myself.

D22: I am depressed that I have lived all my life as if I were highly independent and completely without need. This is not true. I am a fake.

D23: How can I proceed with my life from this point on if I have been an impostor? I shall be found out.

D24: My analyst says I shall have to live a more realistic life – not as a god, nor as a shit – and this is a bummer. He says I'm getting towards ordinary depression and he even seems amused by it, the son of a bitch.

D25: Life is what it is and I am what I am. I am not so bad, nor am I so good. I have my ups and my downs. I might have said 'I wish this were not so' – but that's life, isn't it?

Once he had finished, the analyst was mildly elated – but this was short-lived, as he could see that his colleagues were slightly aghast. Was this really necessary, asked Sally Forensic; was he really suggesting, she wondered, that these 'Ds', as he called them, were chronologically linked? The analyst replied that this indeed was the whole point: each patient had a different thread, like a sort of psychic DNA of depression, and it was actually rather beautiful once you studied it. Before Sally could say another word, the analyst was already praising depression as a remarkable emotion, surely more sophisticated and more deeply human than anxiety, anger or elation.

William Glastonbury, unlike Sally, was more than up to this kind of list, and felt that the analyst had left out some crucial steps.

'For example,' he explained, looking at his notes, 'after D6, when you say that your patient was depressed because she was alone, you forgot to include the depression that occurs when someone attacks their objects and as a result of this denigration the object world feels depleted and empty. "X" was furious with "A", and with all others, and was able to leave her job without further ado because these people were beneath her contempt; but now that she had reduced the people she had previously valued into non-entities, she was without internal nurturance and this would have contributed to her depression.'

Carson jumped in and said he thought the analyst should add to D8, when the patient felt depressed out of the blue, the fact that anxiety plays a cascading role in all depressions. He pointed out that once the patient was without internal support there was a panic attack because she felt *genuinely* abandoned – so, oddly enough, at this point depression was acting as a form of anti-anxiety agent. When people reached this stage of depression, Carson continued, they were on the verge of losing their sense of self, and being depressed was a way of re-embodying the self at a moment when anxiety threatened one's sense of being. The psychoanalyst agreed with Carson's view, saying that he had often noted how at this stage people would hold themselves and seek depression – usually with arms folded across the stomach, as if to emphasise the fact that at least this slumped self was still on the earth.

Sally Forensic pointed out that with D9 there was a paranoid cure through false diagnosis. Once the person was told that the cause of their state of mind was x, whatever x was, there was an initial sense of relief – 'I knew it was something.' She recalled the days when everyone was thought to have some form of temporal lobe epilepsy: when sufferers were told they had TLE, so slight that they didn't even know it, they were elated, just as today people loved to be told they were suffering from post-traumatic stress disorder. The problem, she added, was that paranoid solutions work for a few moments before it unconsciously dawns on the self that these single definitions have unwittingly eliminated the remainder of the person's personality, gutting them of all other contributors to personal meaning.

Other members of the group pointed out that with D12–14 the analyst had not included the logic of regression in depression. They argued – and the psychoanalyst agreed – that by that point the sufferer had lost 'higher level' functions and was living in what they called a 'pocket regression', which simply meant they were now suffering from substantially diminished adult functioning. People in this state were now unable to remember the simplest of things, they failed to show up to meetings, they forgot social engagements, and so on.

The psychoanalyst added that he thought he had left something else out: this was also the time when internal conversation changed. While it was true that the depressed self tended to engage in a ritualised type of inner discourse, there were other sorts of conversation which lived outside the zone, so to speak. But the logic of depression led to a gradual erosion of these other forms of inner conversation, and so the self progressively lost the help of other parts of the personality that seemed to have lost their voice.

By the end of the evening the group agreed that depression was, after all, a marvellous thing.

The analyst was well into his walk home, still thinking over the discussion, when his musing was rudely interrupted. He ran into Fred Murk, his comedian friend, who was reeling home from a dinner party. It would be an understatement to say that Murk hailed the analyst; he practically assaulted him on the street and the analyst knew there was no escape. It would be at least fifteen minutes before he would get to his front door, even if Murk did not insist they sit down on the ground, Godot-like under a tree, to talk about 'issues'.

'So what the fuck are you looking so glum about?' yelled the comedian.

'Look, don't shout, for Christ's sake – you'll wake everyone up.'

'What, at fucking eleven o'clock in the evening? Who goes to bed this early, anyway?'

'Well, I do . . . ordinarily,' said the analyst.

'Yeah, well, you're one depressed dude, aren't you?'

'Oh rubbish. Anyway, if I am depressed then I'm very happy about it. I think depression is wonderful: glorious even.'

'What, are you pissed?'

'No, I'm fine actually,' replied the analyst. 'Just come from the Discussion Group. So I am utterly sober.'

'Oh, so you've been with your colleagues, your colleagues, have you?'

'Yes, Murk, I have been talking to people other than myself. Quite nice really.'

'So tell me,' yelled Murk, 'why is it that so many

beautiful women who train to be Kleinian psychoanalysts become ugly?'

The analyst was completely startled by this. 'What the hell do you mean?'

'Tell me why beautiful women turn into depressed sacks when they qualify as Kleinians.'

'What on earth are you talking about?'

Murk launched into a rambling explanation. 'Well, while you were . . . apparently celebrating depression with your friends . . . I had the horrid misfortune to be at a party with some of your other colleagues, and I sat next to this woman with fading blonde hair – about forty-two, I'd say. I could see she had once been beautiful, but now she was on the way to being ugly. Not completely there, but on the way. You know, you could tell that at one time she didn't give a damn what she said, but now she's become so fucking cautious. So cautious. It affects the mouth. Mouth caution – the psychoanalytic disease. "Watch what you say!" hears the mouth, so of course eventually it curls down. As the mouth curls down the nose sticks out, because it's trying to rise above this deficit, and caught in this conflict the eyes drop to the feet or wander off to the side, while the forehead crinkles in agony. It's fucking disgusting what your profession does to beautiful women.'

One of the really irritating things about Murk was that he often got things right, and all too often the analyst found himself opposing something with which he in fact agreed. When Murk pushed the analyst onto a bench outside Snap Out Of It, the photographer's, he knew he was in for a lecture.

'Do you deny what I'm saying?' asked the comedian.

'What good would that do? You want your fun: so go

24

for it. Tell me, why does Kleinian psychoanalysis make women ugly?'

'Because it destroys their narcissism. You've said yourself that they can only be sexy at those awful, godforsaken dances at their conventions, when they all come out on the dance floor like floozies at a can-can competition. Otherwise, they sit all hunched up behind their couches trying to get every poor sod they can into the depressive position. Depression – which you seem to think is so marvellous – is the very thing that ruins desire, destroys bodily narcissism, and kicks the fun out of life. And, of course, their patients fall in love with them because they're out of sight! If they were in view, no such luck.'

Murk moved a few inches further down the bench, away from the analyst, so that he could give the analyst a long, lingering look, with mischief criss-crossing his face. He was clearly delighted with himself, as he knew the analyst agreed with him.

'You agree with me, I can see it!' announced Murk, triumphantly.

'Depression has nothing to do with the depressive position.'

'Oh, and why not?'

'The so-called depressive position is an ambition of the analyst, a kind of programmatic desire, and I agree, analysts who spend their life toiling away to get their patients in this place are—'

'Killing things off, aren't they!'

'No – just being boring,' the psychoanalyst said. 'Just boring.'

'Aha! It's the repetition compulsion, but now it's the

analyst's repetition compulsion. Beyond the pleasure principle, isn't it?'

'Where have you come across these terms? I thought you hated psychoanalysis.'

'I fucking loathe it. But look, man, I live in this part of the city and you can't go to a fucking dinner party without running into an analyst, so you have to learn some of the lingo . . . and anyway, Uva Splinner used those words and I tried to be playful with her, but no luck.'

'You sat next to Uva Splinner?'

'Yeah, she was beautiful once, wasn't she?'

'Yes, very.'

'And then what happened?'

'Oh shut up, Murk. Let's push off.'

The psychoanalyst was disturbed by this conversation because it evoked a memory of one of the many conventions he had attended. In a room full of hundreds of analysts, one of his male colleagues had said, 'Right, look around – now, try to find a beautiful woman.' And at first glance they had all looked plain or strained, or worse: deeply, deeply serious. Yes, that was it. It was the look of studied seriousness. Maybe that was the answer: if you felt that you had to look so serious, maybe thousands of hours of enforced seriousness restructured your face and your body and eventually destroyed beauty. But he knew that this had been one of those awful male bonding moments – clearly misogynist – in which men advanced their intimacy at the expense of women. It was one of those horrid memories, and the analyst hated Murk for his capacity to unearth if not the repressed, the hopefully discarded.

Trying to rescue himself from discomfort, the analyst

wondered: what was beauty, after all? His thoughts returned to the marvels of depression, and he realised that his list of Ds had completely left out the body and the face and the way in which depressed people lost their beauty. But that was not quite it. It was more as if they lost a kind of potential radiance, that glow which emanates from the non-depressed self.

So was Murk partly right?

Was this serious aim of shoving patients into the depressive position a way of destroying human radiance? Was there something about the radiant aspect of ordinary human life that evoked unconscious envy in psychoanalysts, who then decided that the cure was depression? The thought shocked him. In fact, that night he stayed up well beyond his bedtime. Unusually, he had a grappa – though he knew he would pay for it the next day. But the thought would not go away. The thought that maybe at some time in the past psychoanalysts had taken a horribly wrong turn in the road. What if psychoanalysts, ensconced in their chairs, tucked away in small chambers where they attached themselves vicariously to shards of reality, envied their patients the lives lived by the living?

Admittedly, he was deeply troubled by what he perceived as clear signs of a mental illness infiltrating the profession. A colleague of his had even gone out on a limb to declare what it was: it was the 'here and now transference interpretation'. Thus the majority of analysts – for it was now a kind of worldwide conversion experience – interpreted whatever the patient was talking about as if it were a hidden reference to the analyst. So the patient could be talking about buying a washing machine that day, and the analyst would say something like: 'You wonder if I am too old to continue to launder your bad thoughts, and you are thinking you may need a new me.' His colleague had said that this sort of interpretation constituted paranoid thinking: a clear idea of reference. The psychoanalyst had for a long time agreed with this, but the implications were terrifying. He had carried out a search of the analytical literature, in the hope that someone else had written about this alarming trend, but found nothing. He thought that perhaps he was wrong and he had stayed away from his colleague – who, the analyst reckoned, was committing political suicide by expressing these ideas in print. But the thought would not go away.

Indeed, the next morning he called a very close colleague, Brent Woodfellow, and they set up time to talk later in the day.

'Brent, you know all this stuff about the "here and now transference interpretation"?'

'Oh God, that shit. Yes, what about it?'

'It's paranoid, Brent.'

'Of course it is.'

'But it's *wrong*.'

'Of course it's wrong,' said Brent.

'Well, don't you think we should do something about it?'

'Like what?'

'I don't know really,' the analyst said. 'But I have this dreadful feeling that I'm taking part in something which is, in its own way, as sick as the fascist movement. How can we do this to patients?'

'You can't do anything about it. It's life.'

'Do you agree with the fascist movement analogy?'

'Look, there are all kinds of little fascist movements all over the world,' said Brent. 'Probably half the corporations on the planet are operated by little Hitlers who terrorise their staff and who publish manifestos that destroy human individuality in the name of corporate socialism. We think we defeated fascism, but it's not true. It was embodied in Nazism, and we won a war, but we missed the entire point. Fascist thinking – purity through expulsion of complexity – was a twentieth-century political response to the increasing scientific, technological and social complexity. So don't get hung up on the psychoanalytical movement unless you want to claim that it should somehow be free of this illness.'

'But it is wrong if we are paranoid and destroying our analysands' complexity in the interests of simplification.'

'Well, who knows. An awful lot of analysts love this shit. They can't get enough of it. Anyway, maybe fascism of this kind cures. After all, who needs a mind these days?'

'Who needs a mind?'

'Yeah, who needs a mind?' repeated Brent. 'What good does it do us? Look at you. Your mind has come up with the troubling thought that psychoanalysis is now the disease that promotes itself as the cure. What good is that thought? What good has it done you? Did you sleep last night?'

'Not well.'

'Of course not, because this was on your mind.'

'Yes, that's true.'

'I rest my case.'

They ended their conversation soon afterwards, and the analyst went to the fishmonger's, to spend some time gazing in through the window. This was for him the equivalent of his local church or temple, and by now the two brothers who owned the place knew not to ask him inside; he just needed to come and stare at the various fish. He could stand there for as long as fifteen minutes. One of the brothers – he couldn't remember if it was Frank or Fingers – had asked him some years ago what he was doing and the psychoanalyst had said, 'They are so strange: ugly and beautiful at the same time.' The brothers knew that he needed to hang out there for obviously private reasons. But today the analyst was really troubled. He hated conflict (a strange disposition for a psychoanalyst) and he hated to find himself out of sorts with his 'group'; yet he felt that psychoanalysis was headed in a dangerous direction and it bothered him.

As he put his head on his pillow that night, he wondered what his dreams would be and whether tomorrow he would recall any of them. It was rather like queuing up for the theatre without knowing what play one was going to see – indeed, what play one would be asked to take part in – a sometimes hazardous venture that we all went through every night of our lives. He did have one final comforting thought: even if psychoanalysis were to disappear, at least it had rediscovered the significance of our dreams – rather like reopening the theatres in London after the Puritans had shut them down in the seventeenth century.

We would not, the analyst thought, ever lose our dreams again; and like anyone living through difficult times, he found it comforting to know that whatever the reality of our world, to sleep, perchance to dream, was to be offered precious renewals of meaning.

2

So, if all the world's a stage . . . ?

The psychoanalyst was not surprised the next morning when, during their Tuesday walk, Westin Moorgate continued to talk about what had occurred outside Heaven's Buns.

'I don't understand why – and I have *really* been struggling with this – I don't get why my intervention was a mistake.'

'It was the right thing to do, Westin, but twenty years ago – not now. No one likes a "have-a-go hero".'

'But *why not*? I mean, do you realise that Mrs Stottlemeyer actually said something like "the bitch had it coming to her"? Whatever we make of that woman, surely she can't mean that?'

'I expect Mrs Stottlemeyer has been changed by her dream life.'

'What do you mean by that?' This was Westin's clarion warning to the psychoanalyst not to go any further, a signal that he preferred to continue to think within known social contexts. And even though he liked the analyst's pace, both mentally and physically, and enjoyed his off-beat sense of humour, it was always disturbing when he went too far or said things that did not make sense.

'Mrs Stottlemeyer's husband died about six years

ago,' the analyst said, 'and she hasn't been the same since. The reason she's constantly in Heaven's Buns is because she had a dream a few weeks after his death in which he told her he would see her in there for coffee. Since then she has never failed to appear, although clearly she is in a distraught state of mind whenever she visits.' He went on to explain that no one would ordinarily know this kind of thing, except that for some months after his death she kept asking the staff if anyone had seen him there. Mrs Stottlemeyer was a very tall woman, with perfectly formed grey hair, twisted Gaudí-like into something akin to a steel sculpture, and so she was quite intimidating and no one felt that she could really be disagreed with.

'How come everyone else knows about Mrs Stottlemeyer's dream life and not me?' asked Westin. As a journalist he was clearly upset to find himself left out of local news.

'Westin, we have other more important matters to think about, such as whether world leaders are capable of depression.'

'Depression? Capable of depression?'

'Yes, whether they have the capacity for it,' replied the analyst.

'Are you talking about economic depression?'

'No, Westin. That's easy-peasy. I mean emotional depression.'

'I'm sure they get depressed. I mean, look at our leader: he looks like a man who's constantly getting out of a swimming pool after some lager-lout has just shoved him in, suit and all.'

'Yes, he does have the idiot grin of the guy who's always being bullied, but I'm not referring to his personal state of mind – rather to his political function.'

'What, depression as a political function? Whatever are you talking about?' The psychoanalyst and the journalist had now reached the pond where they often rested for a few moments, in the hope that they might spot some of the more exotic wildfowl in the area, but today, although it was beautiful weather, the pond was duck-free.

'Well, we agree that all the world's a stage, yes?'

'I don't agree in advance to anything.'

'Well, pretend you agree,' said the analyst, 'just for discussion's sake. You see, it has a bearing on your question about why people no longer seem to care about ordinary heroic gestures as part of civic life.'

Westin Moorgate was silent as the psychoanalyst continued. He said that he thought that world leaders led people in many senses; that even though countries and their leaders were separate entities, people unconsciously assumed that a country and its leader were one. So if a country, such as 'Superpower' (the name the psychoanalyst and his friends frequently used for America), decided it had a mission to convert the entire world to its particular vision of reality – for the sake of argument, that the world should be a free marketplace for Superpower – and that its best way of getting this idea across was to invade recalcitrant regimes and change them, then folks all over the world watching their TVs would have no option but to conclude that Superpower's solution to any conflict between self and other was to deck the other with as big a punch as possible. 'Shock and awe' was a particular phrase he recalled.

33

'That's what "your Henry" did to you last week,' the analyst said: 'shock and awe.'

Westin was still listening, so the analyst went on. 'The world leaders show us how to behave. And if Superpower decides that the solution to conflict is to beat the shit out of any opposition then it sets the standard. We live in anarchy today because the world has not only lost its meaning – and anarchy is a way of socialising nihilism – but because the idiots who operate Superpower and its flunkies (basically the entire Western world) have not just condoned violence, they have invited it.'

At this point Westin decided to speak up. 'Well what's the alternative? It's a bloody dangerous world out there and Superpower is keeping the hordes away from us. Were it not for Superpower, we would all be in deep shit.'

'No, no, no. It's the other way round. But if Superpower could take its time, look into the causes of violence and terrorism – which, of course, it does not want to do – but if it could, then it could begin to accept partial responsibility for extremism, extremism that it engenders through its own insanely sanctioned state violence.'

'Rubbish,' said Westin. 'But anyway, I'm not talking politics with you, because you promised you would stick to another agenda. Why has all this got anything to do with depression?'

'Because no one is responsible for damage,' said the analyst. 'Superpower can pulverise an entire nation and never be called upon to feel badly about it; and the odd thing about democracy is that it ensures this. Just like a corporation, in which no one is individually responsible for corporate error, democracy guarantees through election that those responsible for damage can be replaced but not held to account.'

'But being replaced *is* being held to account.'

'Only in the narrow political sense. Sure, they're dumped, but then some other idiot takes their place, only to spill out the same tedious platitudes. But meanwhile the other countries on the world stage – especially those that have been and still are being oppressed – receive no form of reparation, there is no apology.'

'But they know how democracy works,' said Westin. 'They can make sense out of Superpower changing a leader, because we are all fed up with him.'

'Yes – but, more importantly, no. They have been damaged, but because emotional life and mental responsibility are not a part of the political remit of any world leader, apology and mental reparation are not features of state-to-state relations.'

'But no one expects that.'

'Of course they do,' said the analyst, 'and that is part of the problem. We thought after Jefferson that there was no point in thinking further about democracy. But replacing a leader as an alternative to mental reparation for the victims of the previous leader leaves the world damaged and unrepaired, and those who are damaged do expect reparation.'

'We are sending money all the time – in fact, too much money, in my view – to the southern countries.'

'Yes, to the Third World. But there is a Fourth World.'

'Oh no, please,' said Westin. 'Don't start making things up.'

The analyst ignored this comment and carried on. 'The Fourth World is composed of all those countries that have experienced Superpower's treatment as a personal violation. However much money is then thrown their way and however many state visits they receive, these countries are in need of mental reparation: either they receive it, or they will bring down the entire world.'

Understandably, Westin Moorgate wanted to know how this kind of reparation could be accomplished – and what was it, anyway?

The psychoanalyst argued that the West was committing massive psychological damage around the globe, creating a Fourth World that no longer correlated with poor and rich nations because it included Canada and Sweden and other wealthy countries. What was needed now was for powerful world leaders to recognise that they really were in a play – a play involving the reality of world affairs – and that how they conducted themselves was crucial. It was all well and good, for example, for a leader to be seen as a folksy, down-home cowboy, the conductor of a well-known symphony orchestra, or the writer of riveting poetry, but what that leader had to understand – and this was crucial to world affairs – was that the way he conducted the country's affairs was his personality. This was him, and if he harmed another country then he had to apologise and commit himself to true reparation.

Westin and the psychoanalyst had to break off their debate as they were now at the southern gate of the park where they customarily split up: Westin to his studio and the psychoanalyst to his consulting room. Their habit was either to high-five gracefully and wordlessly or, occasionally, to knuckle one another. Usually this worked, but today the analyst knuckled while Westin high-fived, which seemed like an unconscious objective correlative of their dispute and their ordinary failures of character. Neither Westin nor the psychoanalyst was any good at greeting or salutation, and now and then they displayed vivid proof of it through these sorts of gestural breakdown. So they left one another embarrassed but also made more honest by this failure.

The psychoanalyst remembered that his first patient, Goran Will, had cancelled and that he actually had an hour in hand to do what he wished. It was a particularly nice day and mornings were so calm and untroubled; in fact, mornings were the psychoanalytical part of a day, when the analyst felt he could begin with a blank screen and slowly project himself into reality, bit by bit without knowing it. So he just wandered about. First he walked up Cone Avenue towards High Tide, his favourite bookshop. He had to be careful as Cone Avenue was somewhere the Teasers of this world preferred to shit, so he walked slowly, watching for turds, but was relieved to find not a single one. Outside High Tide he gazed at the new books in the window. This was ordinarily a visual pleasure, even if he knew he was never going to get around to reading anything. Today, however, one book did strike him: *History: The Depression*, by Mike Paine. The analyst was in the shop like a shot the moment it opened.

As he had so little time to read these days, the analyst had developed the knack of scanning a book in a matter of minutes; in this way he often had the good fortune of happening upon an author's main argument. Rodin's *Thinker* was on the cover and Paine's first chapter was on Proust. It was titled 'Remembrance is depression'. Flipping through the chapters, the analyst got the gist of Paine's thesis: that *if* we choose to convert the past into thought, which Paine argued was 'the work of history', then we have no option but to face our depression. According to Paine, we have a choice. We can simply live with a past unconverted into history, and he presented an eloquent argument for leaving it there, or we can 'attempt the conversion'. Leaving our past unhistoricised – there was a chapter against psychoanalysis on these grounds – is to live without 'pretension'. The analyst thought this a peculiar choice of word, so he lingered about a bit and gathered that Paine was suggesting that an unhistoricised, unconverted past left us without 'pre-tension', without a matrix that would make us tense about our future. He read further:

> We have two choices. If we live out of the past, we are generatively thoughtless in the present and we have no future, so we are without pretensions. If we have converted our past into our history then we are not just burdened by what we choose to recall and to tell ourselves, but in acquiring a history we have opened the avenue for depression, as to recollect any past is to be depressed by it.

Paine believed that the so-called sociopath was someone who elected to be without a history and was therefore unburdened by his past and never subject to depression. Paine's radical argument was that many of the world's great leaders were without historical conversion experiences and functioned as sociopaths, making them far more effective politicians. Those who transformed the past into history were, however, depressed by the act itself – and here Paine was at pains to point out that it was never the content of the recollected that constituted this depression, but the act of history-making itself – and therefore were less efficient leaders in the modern world because they were slower to arrive at decisions in moments of crisis.

That explained why electorates were turning to two new types of world leader, the sexually promiscuous leader and the religious zealot: both had in common a lack of history. The sexual predator, argued Paine, never thought about what he was doing and had to make quick, on-the-spot decisions in the midst of intense instinctual conflict, so he automatically assumed the status of a man who could think in a crisis. The religious zealot left any history up to his God, which meant that one's past was to be interpreted later by a higher authority, so the religious zealot was also free of his own history.

The analyst glanced from page to watch and back again, as he now had only a few more minutes before he had to sprint down the hill to his office. Should he buy this book or not? He could not make up his mind and, like all historically determined selves, he deferred the decision until later – after all, High Tide was just five minutes from his office – so he left the book and arrived in time for his patient.

'You see,' said Hector Veil, 'I don't see the point of all of this.'

'Of all of this?' asked the analyst.

'Yes.'

'What is the "this"?'

'Well, this effort we are supposed to be making,' replied the patient.

'Effort?'

'Well, I don't know how to talk about it, but this effort or work we must all put into making our lives work, or our selves work. It seems such an incredible chore. The whole thing is rather depressing.'

'Depressing?'

'Yes, it's depressing. Nothing is working out.'

'You thought things would be different?' asked the analyst.

'Well, damn right I did. All those years in school labouring away. For what? Where has it got me?'

'I gather it's got you to the point where you wonder why you make the effort.'

'Don't you think that's depressing?'

'To be left with this question?'

'I'm thirty-two,' said Veil, wearily. 'I work sixty hours a week, I have a wife and two kids, and even though I earn a fortune I owe money. I have no time in the evenings to do what I want to do, as I have to stay late in the office or I'll get the push. My wife and I fuck once every three or four weeks, which sucks. I love my kids – don't get me wrong – but, Jesus Christ, you call this a life?'

'In what way did you think it would or could be different?'

'Sorry?'

'You thought it could be different from this?'

'I . . . well, of course I did.'

'Correct me please if I am wrong,' said the analyst, 'but as I recall, you decided in your early twenties to go into corporate law, knowing that you would often be working all night long, sometimes for days on end. You married your wife knowing that she was a banker who would also keep very long hours. You both wanted to earn a million a year and retire in your early forties.'

'Yes, that's about right.'

'Well that is rather depressing, isn't it?'

'What, because that was or is my view of how to live my life?' Veil's tone became sour. 'I thought analysts weren't meant to pass judgement.'

'I mean,' explained the analyst, 'driving yourself that hard, amongst other things, would naturally be rather depressing, wouldn't it?'

'I would have thought it would be rewarding.'

'In a Faustian sort of way, at first, yes – but for how long would this work?'

'Well,' replied Veil, 'obviously I think, and so do a lot of other people, that this is the way to conduct a life. I know it's hard work – I don't see enough of the family, and so on – but there is something else.'

'What comes to mind?'

'Disappointment . . . that's what comes to mind.'

'What disappoints you?'

'I don't know really, but . . .' Hector Veil paused thoughtfully. 'Setting aside what we've just been talking about, I am not the sort of man I thought I would be. My life is not measuring up to what I expected. I saw things differently some time ago.'

'So perhaps the problem was in the original expectation.'

'I expected to make millions and . . .'

'You have – so?'

'So . . . I don't know what the problem is.'

'So there would *appear* to be a lack of knowledge over an important matter.'

'You make it sound problematic,' said Veil, 'as if I know something but don't want to know what I know. Is that it?'

'In our work together you've let me know that you set very high standards for yourself as a young man, and that you envisioned yourself in a particular way.'

'Oh, you mean my BMW, beautiful wife, fabulous house . . . and the tons of things I wanted.'

'Yes, the tons, tons of things you wanted,' replied the analyst.

'You have emphasised "tons".'

'Great word, isn't it? Sort of sounds like it is.'

'So . . . I wanted too much?'

'I think so,' the analyst said. 'In fact, I think your self-expectation was a form of greed and that your depression is an expression of disappointment that you have not received the tons of goodies your ideal self promised you, especially as you were putting in the long hours and making the sacrifices.'

'But why would this depress me?'

'Well, it's not that you've decided this is too material a vision of life – although personally speaking, I would agree that it is. It is more that *unless* you received all that you had unconsciously promised yourself, then you would be a failure; and, as you have not received everything, then you are a failure – no matter how much it appears that you have everything.'

'What, because I don't have the yacht and the timeshare in the West Indies?'

'No, because you do not have happiness. You were promised a state of mind and a form of well-being that is not even on the horizon.'

For a long time Hector Veil lay in silence. The psychoanalyst had been unusually talkative. Both were no doubt taken by this fact, and silence now seemed the best place for the analysis to go. Veil did recognise that in his early twenties he had arrogantly assumed that life in the meritocracy would bring riches beyond belief, and that he could acquire states of mind through material accomplishment: a kind of Zen in reverse. He thought about the analyst's use of the word 'greed'. He hated hearing this and for a while it rang in his mind like some sort of accusation – 'you greedy bastard' or 'greedy, greedy, greedy' or 'greedy guts'– but when he recovered from this choral response and actually thought about what the psychoanalyst had said, he felt a strange kind of freedom. It seemed simply true. He was depressed not because he was not getting what one could get in life – he had more than most, by far – but because he was failing to fulfil the standards he had set for himself in the beginning of his career, standards that were not ambitious, but greedy. That greed had gutted him of all the other parts of the self – parts that could have spent time in a different way, setting other sorts of goals – and in so doing he had lost touch not simply with his kids and his wife, but more importantly with himself.

The psychoanalyst, thinking along similar lines in these remaining minutes of the analytical hour, pondered how Veil's depression would have to have another D number assigned to it. This particular despair had to do with greed displacing reality and simultaneously eliminating other parts of the personality.

After Hector Veil departed, the psychoanalyst pursued this line of thought. He felt that the world was in the grip of greed, a frame of mind that inhabited Veil and also seemed to be the engine of world politics. He opened his notebook and began to write some of these ideas down.

> We are all caught up in a worldwide depression – not the economic kind, but the worst kind: we have lost human value. And what is that? It is not the value that we place on ourselves as a narcissistic action, but the value that derives from our existence. On that you cannot cheat. How long are we here? Sixty years, seventy, eighty? And during our generation how often are we complicitous in crimes against humanity? Thinking about the greenhouse effect is essential, but concrete. Because we have lost the unconscious – or it has left us – we cannot see the psychic greenhouse effect, how our self-inflated state, our greed, gives rise not merely to literal over-consumption, but to the degradation of the mental economy, so we now have only flatulent discourse.

The psychoanalyst was rather shocked by these last words. Nonetheless he continued to write:

We wish to know nothing of ourselves, except
the bare necessities. Hence our interest in
neuroscience instead of the life of the mind.
This is strip mining. Now we are returned to
the shallows of fundamentalism in any form,
because we have refused insight and are left
with unbridled greed, arrogant narcissism,
and mindlessness. I think I shall call this the
'Fundamentalist Return' in acknow-
ledgement of the regression that has occurred
in our civilisation due to our eradication of
the Freudian project. With no meaningful
structure for looking into ourselves – except,
God help us, the concrete notion that we can
locate thought through the PET scan – we
have all become fundamentalists. And what
does that mean? It means that we are reduced
to the fundamentals, the beginnings.
According to that logic, there are good people
and bad people. Of course, this isn't up to us.
It's the Great Bugger in the sky – depending
on which religion we choose – who decides
it. So we become 'children' once again, but
now of course back to 'children of God'. We
have lost the Freudian child who was sexual,
competitive, capable of murder, compelled
to accept personal responsibility at great
mental cost, sponsored by mental challenges
to fulfil high human ideals such as repairing
damage committed against another through
the sense of guilt, or listening to what the

other said because listening is a natural part of relating to the other. No, none of this for the new children of God. Born again in the fundamentalist world, we are free to split life into the loved and the hated. We are free from the burdens of human evolution and we can all return to our origins, to our fundamentals. And, of course, reduced to such intended limits, we need looking after again by the Great Bugger in the clouds.

The psychoanalyst was momentarily exhilarated to have written these words. He stood up for a moment, glanced at his page, and punched his fist to the sky as if he had achieved some kind of victory. Alas, the moment was short-lived, and – as he might have expected – he began to feel a bit low. It was 10.30 and he had a break in his schedule, so to offset the progression of mood – towards depression – he headed to Hippo for a coffee.

The staff were a bit perplexed to see him, as he usually did not show up until 12.45, so there was a murmuring of 'What are you doing here? Everything all right?' But Cassandra, the experienced and rather beautiful manager, said that she was sure he must have a cancellation, and what would he like: single or double espresso? Cassandra was never in a hurry and knew the psychoanalyst well enough to be aware that sometimes he could be thrown by the simplest question. On this occasion she could see that he did not know which of the two to go for, so she simply said, 'Back in a mo.' When she returned, about five minutes later, he said he would like a sparkling water.

'Sparkling water it is!' she chimed.

The water arrived shortly afterwards with a piece of lemon in it. The analyst tried to fish it out. Cassandra noticed this and said, 'Oh, sorry, forgot: you don't like it with lemon, do you?'

Actually the analyst found lemon in sparkling water just shy of obscene. He had conducted numerous imaginary conversations with anonymous waiters over the years which went something along the following lines.

'You don't like lemon in your sparkling water?'

'Well, would you like a log in your bathtub?'

'I beg your pardon?'

'Why would I want a lemon in my sparkling water?'

'Because it scents the water.'

'Then I would have asked for sparkling water with lemon.'

'You seem so cross.'

'I am, because if you try drinking it, and do have one on me, each time you try to take a sip of water this log bumps into your lips, obstructing the simple act of drinking. Go on, try it – try drinking your water without the lemon crashing into your mouth.'

According to this imaginary conversation, the waiter would be momentarily bewildered. And that, of course, was what was so gratifying about these imaginary conversations, or daydreams, because the other was usually beaten (although even in the privacy of this inner life the analyst felt bad about being a bully).

So there he was, Cassandra giving him a new glass and new water, and he felt like some kind of idiot king. He was not exactly on the way to feeling better – that was for sure. Psychoanalysts, he realised, did not talk or write much about daydreaming. It was like this big 'no go' area: although they discussed unconscious phantasies, this was not the same. No. A place where we spend an awful lot of our time – dreaming by day – was obviously deeply embarrassing. To his astonishment and chagrin, he realised he had never actually asked after a patient's daydreaming; nor had his own analyst ever asked him about his daydreaming. Freud didn't duck the subject, though he rather saw it as simple wish-fulfilment. The psychoanalyst wasn't so sure about this. If they were simple wish-fulfilments, why weren't we asking after the fulfilled wishes of the day?

He was deep into this sort of research when Val Vacto popped her head through the café door, asked him if he was free, and then joined him. This pleased the psychoanalyst, as he was always glad to see her. When the academic asked him what he was up to, he explained that he was struck by the fact that psychoanalysis did not seem interested in daydreams; he mentioned that he had just been having one, and recounted it to her. Val, whom he loved because she was always game, said that was nothing: fifteen minutes before, when some arrogant bastard stepped in front of her in the queue at High Tide, she took out a knife, cut his balls off, and stuffed them in his mouth.

Val's eyes were alight with a certain kind of psychic fire, and clearly she wanted the analyst to volley. So he said that he had imagined smashing someone in the face that morning when he was turning the corner by Medici, the Tile Store, and the guy forced him to virtually flatten himself against the wall of the building.

'You smashed him in the face?'

'Yeah.'

'Did you knock him off his feet?'

'Yeah.'

'Did he scream in agony?'

'No, not actually . . .' The analyst felt he might have failed in the game.

'Why not?'

'Jesus, Val, it didn't occur to me.'

'Well, maybe you knocked the stuffing out of him and he couldn't make a peep.'

'Yeah, I suppose so.'

'But my guys always yell. You should have heard the sound the guy made when I cut his balls off!'

Cassandra, passing by at this moment, overheard Val's comment. 'You cut someone's balls off?' she asked, in disbelief.

Unfortunately for all three of them, Cassandra had a Wagnerian voice that could be heard at a hundred metres, and about ten people – both in Hippo and outside – overheard the manager's astonishment.

'Did you hear that?' said one.

'My God,' said another. 'She's cut someone's balls off!'

'Has someone just cut off someone's balls?'

'Where?'

'In Hippo.'

'Oh my God. That's terrible.'

'What's terrible?'

'A terrible thing in Hippo. Someone's in there with a knife, cutting off men's balls.'

'Should we call the police?'

'I've got a mobile . . . Yes, please come quick, there's a mad woman in Hippo who has cut off a customer's balls – she's attacking everyone . . . Yes, Hippo, the coffee shop, right next to the bank on the High Street . . . No, I haven't seen it, I can't see anything because of the crowd. I know they shouldn't be, but everyone is curious. I think it's one person . . . My name? My name is Meredith Monrovia.'

'Excuse me, are you Meredith Monrovia?'

'Yes.'

'The one who does the soap commercials on the telly?'

'Yes, that's me.'

'Wow, that's pretty cool. Is the pay good?'

'Well, it pays the bills and—'

'So what's going on in Hippo?'

'Oh God, some woman's gone nuts and cut off some poor bastard's balls with a knife.'

'Are you sure?'

'Well, I didn't see it myself, but that's what I heard.'

'Because I thought they were serving sheep's balls this evening.'

'Sheep's balls?'

'Well, I don't know, but that's what I think I heard.'

'When did you hear that?'

'Well, I'm not sure exactly, but I got a pretty clear impression.'

'Oh fuck.'

'What?'

'I've just called the police!'

'What, about sheep's balls?'

'No, about the woman who's cutting them off.'

'But maybe she works in the kitchen.'

'Oh shit. That's right. Why didn't I think of the obvious? I've just gone along with the herd, haven't I? What should I do?'

'Well Meredith, I think you're great, and anyway you can't do anything now, and you . . . Why don't we just get out of here? It's none of our business. And this is a huge crowd now, isn't it? So the police should be here.'

Meredith Monrovia and her fan dashed up the hill in the nick of time. Within seconds three police cars had pulled up in front of Hippo; constables jumped out, quickly dispersing the crowd. They rushed into the café and were confronted by a completely empty space. Officers ran downstairs to the kitchen, checked out the men's and women's loos, and looked under the tables, but no one was to be found. The sergeant raised the alarm: it looked as if there had been serious trouble, and the attacker may very well have abducted the staff at knifepoint. He ordered two officers to search the premises for human testicles; they quickly put on their protective gloves as the other members of the force moved up and down the High Street, taking the usual one-two-three-step approach to imagined but as yet un-encountered danger.

One can only imagine the terror of the psychoanalyst, Val and Cassandra, who were observing this scene from the analyst's office window. Val had her hand mirror out and they could see the squad moving up and down the street.

'For God's sake, what am I going to do?' asked Cassandra, evidently thinking of her boss. 'Gideon's going to kill me!'

'You haven't done anything,' said the analyst.

'I've left the scene of a crime.'

'There was no crime,' he said.

'Well, I've left Hippo empty.'

'I think you should go back,' said Val.

'Yes, quickly,' added the psychoanalyst.

'But what am I going to say?'

'Well . . .' said the analyst, 'tell them you were just taking out the rubbish.'

'But what do I say about the crime?'

'There wasn't a crime!' shrieked Val.

'But they all think there was,' continued Cassandra. 'Isn't it giving false witness? Surely I'm guilty of inciting a riot or something?'

'No, you just reported a daydream,' said Val.

'Please come with me – hey, you're an analyst, you can explain it to them.'

'Well, I don't know,' said the psychoanalyst, now further alarmed by this vision of talking to the police.

'No, please,' said Cassandra, 'both of you come and explain this, so that I don't get sacked.'

Val Vacto looked at the analyst and they both agreed they had better return to Hippo and face the music, although they weren't quite clear what the melody might be. As they walked back and people in the crowd recognised them, they tried to appear as ordinary as they could – which was difficult, as they were terrified.

Cassandra walked in first and said 'Hi guys' to the five constables in the café, two of whom were on their knees, searching under the table for a pair of testicles and possibly a penis. She asked if she could help them, while Val and the psychoanalyst sat down at one of the tables as if they were waiting to be served. One of the policemen called the sergeant on a walkie-talkie. In moments his superior arrived and told them they had to leave, as this was a crime scene. Cassandra explained some of what had happened and it was clear that the police were deeply perplexed.

'So what do you mean, "a daydream"?' the sergeant asked Val.

'I was just telling this man here about a daydream I'd had,' she replied, as the sergeant's gaze crossed the table.

'And who are *you*?'

'A psychoanalyst.'

'A what?'

'A p-s-y-c-h—'

'Oh yeah, okay. But what are you doing here?'

'What, now?' the analyst asked.

'What are you doing out of your office?'

'I was having a coffee,' he explained.

'You have coffee with your patients while they tell you their daydreams?'

'She isn't my patient.'

The sergeant turned back to Val. 'So, madam, just what do you think you were doing telling this man that you had cut off another man's balls?'

'I didn't do that. I had a daydream about it, that's all.'

'That's all? *That's all?* You reckon it's no big deal to think of cutting off a man's balls and reporting it, just like that?'

By now the crowd, some fifteen people, had quietly infiltrated the front part of Hippo and were clearly fascinated by the unfolding confrontation.

'Well, I have this daydream quite a lot actually,' said Val. 'In fact, so do most women.'

'What! Do you have any idea what this means?' asked the sergeant, as his officers nodded knowingly.

'No, not exactly,' replied Val, with a worried look. She shot a quick glance at the analyst, who was now fascinated by his watch.

'It means you are spreading a vicious story about the fine women of this country, that's what it means. I shall certainly be looking this up in the book when I'm back at the station. I am sure this is an offence.'

'What, reporting a daydream?'

'Why do we have theatres?' asked the sergeant. He was standing taller now that he was making a point, even though he had no clue about the answer.

The psychoanalyst suddenly rejoined the conversation. 'So that staged dreams can be kept on reservations, like Native American Indians,' he suggested.

'Exactly,' said the relieved sergeant. He addressed Val again: 'And so you know what you've done?'

'Strayed off the reservation?'

'You have offended public boundaries. If you think so highly of your daydreams, why not put on a play? You could even call it *Off With Their Balls*.' At this, his colleagues roared with laughter, as did the crowd.

'Actually,' said Val, 'I have written a play that was produced at Vagina Hall, and it was called *Dick The Dicks*.'

There was absolute silence in the café. The first signs of movement were the glances from the officers toward the sergeant. Val had not consciously realised that cops were sometimes called 'dicks', but the psychoanalyst could feel it coming before Val's title left her lips (and he briefly found himself contemplating the phrase 'private dick'). He had been

54

to see Val's play, which really was quite good, although he did find her fascination with what she called 'genithalia' a bit much. ('Genithalia' was an oblique reference to the work of Sándor Ferenczi, who argued in his book *Thalassa* that when people fucked, the penis represented the human species' effort to return to the sea from which we all originated.)

The sergeant eventually broke the silence. 'What do you mean, *Dick The Dicks*?'

'You really want me to tell you about my play?' asked Val, with something close to a renewed sense of mischief crossing her face. But the sergeant was now clearly starting to feel that he was involved in a farce, and he abruptly ended the confrontation by telling his men that this was a first, but that it was not atypical of events in this part of the city. He ordered the crowd to either sit down and order, or leave the premises. As he left, he glared at Hippo's façade, as if somehow the building were to blame for the incidents inside; Val told the analyst she thought he was double-checking to make sure that it wasn't a theatre after all.

The analyst absolutely hated the word 'processing' but he and Val judged this to be what they were doing as they spent the next hour talking about what had happened. Val said the remark about theatre was rather depressing, but true, and the analyst said that perhaps the same applied to daydreams – but oddly enough, he still could not understand why they weren't reported in analysis. Val, who was one of the great feminist analytical scholars of her era, reckoned that the daydream had been usurped by what Freud called 'the dream proper', and so relegated to psychoanalytic oblivion. Dreams were highbrow experiences, while daydreams were pop culture, and this Freud was not interested in.

Val had to go off to buy vegetables for her fortnightly soup group so the analyst returned to his office, reopened his notebook and read a few of his most recent thoughts on depression. He realised that he was a bit depressed himself and wondered what the possible link might be. What had he just been thinking about? Daydreams. So, he wondered to himself, is it that we cannot live our daydreams? That could not be: some of them would be so embarrassing or absurd – who would want to do such a thing? He had also been thinking of the theatre, but what possible connection was resident in that idea? We have no place to portray our daydreams? That seemed closer to the crux of the matter. We have no place to put them on, so to speak. And psychoanalysis did not want them. So there were mental zones still declined by psychoanalysis. Was this why he was feeling depressed?

Time passed and he thought on.

Perhaps it was that daydreaming was an object of contempt. Winnicott had argued that 'fantasysing', as he called it, was alternative to creativity, but the analyst had never believed this to be true. No, it seemed that psychoanalysis had decided that daydreaming was not worth the effort of consideration; but he kept in reserve the thought that it was also a matter of embarrassment. He decided to call William Glastonbury.

'Hello. What's up?'

'I'm thinking about why we don't talk about daydreams.'

'Too shallow.'

'What is shallow about them?' asked the analyst.

'Well . . . they fulfil simple wishes, sexual or aggressive.'

'But we should be interested in that sort of thing.'

'Yeah,' said Glastonbury, 'but it's conscious stuff: nothing really unconscious going on.'

'But Freud said it was a form of playing.'

'So?'

'Well, aren't we denying ourselves some kind of play space?'

'Not really. We play. We just keep it to ourselves.'

'Well, that seems rather sad to me,' said the analyst.

'What, you think we should be telling people that we have been playing?'

'Well . . . why not?'

'Because who would be interested?'

'No one is interested?'

'The last time anyone was interested,' said Glastonbury, 'was in your childhood – when Tom or Becky or Bob or Alice dropped by and called out "want to come out to play?" '

'That's awful.'

'What?'

'It's true,' explained the analyst. 'That *was* the last time anyone asked me out to play.'

'So now you have to play by yourself.'

'No wonder daydreams are full of sex, aggression or lonely heroics.'

'What do you mean?'

'Well, we can't do something we used to love doing, and so now we're pissed off. We're left as kind of lonesome heroes longing for the sexuality of playing.'

'There is no sexuality to playing,' said Glastonbury confidently. 'That's a confusion.'

'There has to be.'

'That would be perversion.'

'No, I don't mean ritualised play, I mean the pleasure of someone dropping by and asking me if I want to run outside and join in. That's just an awful lot of fun, or it was, and we can't do that now.'

'Well, get over it.'

'Yes, but I'm thinking about depression these days and I reckon that one of the reasons we're all bummed is that no one asks us out to play. We can't just drop everything and run out into the streets and invent something.'

'Okay big guy, if I dropped by your office and said "want to come out to play?" exactly what game would you like us to invent?'

The psychoanalyst was stumped. He had no idea. Glastonbury pointed out that he had obviously lost his capacity for playing, so it was no good pining over a lost possibility. It was only after the analyst had put the phone down that an idea did pop into his head: if Glastonbury had invited him out to play, they might have played terrorists and counter-terrorists. He could have been a terrorist trying to blow up a building. No, that didn't seem right, he didn't like that scenario . . . He could be a counter-terrorist who apprehended Glastonbury, who was just about to blow up Viyella Lampworth (a close colleague he fancied). The analyst would heroically rescue Viyella from Glastonbury and then the game would be all over.

'But we would look like complete idiots,' said Viyella when the analyst told her the idea later that day.

'Why?'

'What, we just run out into the street and play this game as adults, and expect not to look like utter fools?'

'Well,' said the psychoanalyst, a bit stumped. 'I guess we would have to . . . ah . . . I know.'

'What?'

'We would have to be no different from anyone else. *Everyone* would have to be doing this on and off during the day, so that we could all play and then we wouldn't look like idiots because it would be normal.'

'But what's the point?' she asked.

'The point is to play.'

'Well, go to the theatre, then.'

'No, Viyella, that won't work. I know, I can predict what you're going to say: you're going to say that the theatre is our play space. But why watch other people doing what we want to do? I don't want to sit watching it, I want to take part, and I don't want to watch something which is scripted like that.' After a slight pause, the analyst added: 'Anyway, the theatre has always depressed me.'

'Oh really, why?'

'Well, I suppose because I feel I've been robbed. I mean, that must be the connection, although I'd not made it till now. We can't play any more: only professional actors get to do that. We can't play football: only professionals get to do that. We can't conduct symphonies: only professionals get to do that. We can't—'

Viyella suddenly piped up: 'When did you ever conduct a symphony?'

'Well, I never have.'

'So you haven't lost anything then, have you?'

59

'Yes, but I've *played* doing it. My brothers and I and some friends, we had an imaginary orchestra and I was the conductor. I reckon I was the Furtwängler of my gang.'

Viyella was somewhat amused by this, especially as she had been married to a professional musician and had always kidded the psychoanalyst about being what she called a 'keen amateur listener'. But after their conversation, when she returned to her consulting room, she thought about the psychoanalyst and what he had been saying, and she thought he might be on to something. Freud certainly did argue that we are discontent with the process of civilisation because we have to give up all kinds of instincts as part of our collaboration with the superego. We could not – could we? – just run out into the streets and play games. In fact, if we did, we could get into serious trouble, especially if we decided to play the psychoanalyst's terrorist game, because the real police might happen by and a serious misunderstanding could ensue. She had read in the paper how an Irish therapist had been stopped by Immigration entering America, and when asked what he did he said he was a 'therapist'; but of course, being Irish, it came out sounding like 'terrorist' and the Immigration Officer was stunned.

Viyella e-mailed the analyst: 'I think you're right about this in a way. We're depressed because we have all had to give up playing together and we have delegated this to professionals. I see now why my comment that you are a keen amateur listener is so offensive. I violated your other self that in play is a great conductor.'

The psychoanalyst e-mailed right back: 'Thanks Viyella. I agree. We have given playing away and we think that genital primacy is enough to substitute for it.'

Viyella wanted to know what he meant, and in his subsequent message the psychoanalyst went on about how fucking was supposed to take the place of playing. He riffed a bit on the notion of 'foreplay' and said it was the only play permitted these days, and it was unfortunate that it was conscripted into the logic of intercourse – we should be able to foreplay any old time we wanted.

Walking home from the office that evening, passing by Snap Out Of It, he wondered if the world's politics were a kind of playing; a horrid, awful, terrible kind of playing, but perhaps something essential. Perhaps we needed an unscripted play, a play of sex, violence and group life: play time in which we were not just alone and daydreaming. Maybe we – all of us in this world of ours – were depressed because we had been forced to give up something we could not give up. Maybe we needed the mayhem of world violence because it gave us pleasure.

What a hell of a thought to have, he mused, as he opened the front door and stepped into his house for another night of domestic life.

3

In the Maze

The psychoanalyst had been avoiding mirrors. Not as a deliberate act of consciousness, but over time – especially this morning, for example – he had begun to take note of it. It was, for him, an embarrassing admission. The simple, unadorned fact was that at sixty-four he saw a figure not exactly to his liking.

Why avoid the mirror?

He was tall, although something less than his original six feet and four inches. He had once cut what he believed to be a striking figure, and had rather towered over his friends. Even though this was not an act of psychological volition, it was undeniable that it gave him pleasure to look down on others, especially other men. Now he was less than himself.

Yet it wasn't shrinkage that bothered him so much as the detail of what he saw in the mirror, on close inspection.

There were liver spots, awful signifiers, marking his hands and his face. When he went for a haircut some weeks earlier the hairdresser, whom he had known for some ten years, mistook a liver spot just above his right eyebrow for the eyebrow itself and asked the analyst if he wanted it 'touched up', before realising his error. But the analyst had thought to himself at the time: 'Fuck it, who gives a shit? Old man, just get on with it – stop trying to turn things back.'

When he had recounted this to a female friend – and at his age he was less and less inclined to talk to other men about his body – she had said: 'Nonsense, you're a good-looking man, so why talk like an undertaker wondering how to prepare a body for a grieving congregation?' When he had put it to his wife in different terms, her response was: 'Well, love, it's not a problem. There's a cream called – I think it's called Out Spot – that will remove the liver spots.' It had been like someone telling him there really was a fountain of youth.

'You mean Byrons The Chemist carries this stuff?'

'I'm sure they do.'

'Will you come with me when I ask for it?'

'Of course I will. Don't be such a fusspot!'

He hated that word. 'Fusspot' produced a rather bizarre complex of associations for him: he imagined 'fuss' as a species of moss, then 'fusspot' as a kind of sexual action, then a self stewed in its own anxiety – a pot full of the self's fuss. As he had something of a weak stomach, he found this rather nauseating.

Reassuring as it was to know that something could take away his liver spots, he knew that was cheating, if these spots were of time. His father had had them and he could recall that when his father was in his mid-sixties he would look at all those spots on his hands; they appeared as signifiers of his father as a kind of soldier marching into the future. They were, the analyst reckoned, signs of the self's engagement with death, which was casting its shadow on beautiful hands that had once been young.

Well, Out Spot might eliminate that part of the heroism of facing death, but he had his doubts. In certain cynical moments – after a glass of red wine or two – he was capable of thinking that someone such as himself should walk about the streets in a T-shirt with a slogan like 'Old Fart' or 'Can't Be Recycled' or 'Hazard To The Eyes'.

On the very rare occasions when he examined his face closely, the wrinkles on his forehead now looked like death's etchings, the nose chock-full of hair. (What was a man supposed to do, advertise for a nose-mower?) The bags under the eyes now seemed like tear receptacles, waiting to catch the endless stream of griefs to come.

He found himself thinking that as great theorists of the mirror, Winnicott and Lacan were, if not completely wrong, only a bit right. For Winnicott, mamma the mirror reflects our true self, which we later discover to be substantially her creation. Initially the world as we know it is our oyster, and we are led to believe that we create reality; hence Winnicott believes that our mother licenses the strength of her child being itself. Lacan, on the other hand, says that we look in the mirror as toddlers (at a stage when we are mentally fragmented) with a very different notion. Mother looks at our image and says 'Pina', or whatever name is assigned to us, so we see an image which we therefore take, by appearance and by name, to be us. But while this external picture is united and clear, internally we are jumbled and utterly unclear.

So much for the mirror catastrophes of the infant.

What about the rest of life?

What about, thought the psychoanalyst, the times – the tens of thousands of times – when the adolescent looks into the mirror? Well, Lacan may be right. He says the self-looking is 'le corps morcelé', the body in pieces, and the self-viewed is 'le moi', the self as a kind of perfect image. But wait a minute! Adolescence surely begins to bridge the gap. What about the fact that at night, before going off to bed, we look at a face well scrubbed and soaped, and we wake up in the morning to a pimple? Not just a pink dot on the face, but a dot with a white Matterhorn-type snow cap? What about this: a body in pieces that we inescapably see in the mirror?

Did Lacan ever address this?

Of course not.

Psychoanalysis never wants to address the rest of human life, he thought. That's why our theory uses the infant or the toddler, because what can they possibly say in objection?

'Well no, actually, I *don't* experience life as bifurcated between the good and bad breast, because in fact—'

'What the hell do you know?' the analysts would reply. 'Anyway, you are preverbal, so shut the fuck up.'

But adolescence: face ruining the potential space of a perfectly good day? Where was Winnicott's mother then, mused the analyst, when she was really needed? Well . . . perhaps not necessarily so far away, he recalled. His elder brother (more handsome than him), for whom days hung on the fate of his face, would scream in the morning as he gazed into the mirror; mother would rush upstairs, towels and equipment in hand, to bathe him and reassure him that all was well and that he was gorgeous and fine. The psychoanalyst as an adolescent had had no such capability. It would have done him a world of good to yell about things like this, but he suffered in silence. He would glance in the mirror, get the picture, and then duck out of sight. If the pimple was really horrifying, he did one of two things: he might cake it over with some sort of lotion or he might actually put a plaster over it. But when he or his brother – or any other sod – went to school on such a day, the result was always the same. 'Oh ho! Look who has a zit this morning. Man, what a big one!' And everyone would crowd around.

What mirror stage theory actually helps a human soul out at a moment like this? Why waste time on the preverbals, who haven't a shit of an idea about this anyway, when the adolescents are stuck right in the heart of the matter?

But he was diverging and he knew it. He had made a rather Freudian slip – not the generic type, but one specific to himself as a Freudian. He had looked into the mirror for a bit too long. That was a mistake. He saw, then, the face of an old man. Move over corps morcelés, he thought. What is this? Body in pieces? In a way. More like body on its way to the rubbish bin, he thought. So now, mirror, what have you got to say? I won't bother with 'Mirror, mirror, on the wall, who is the fairest of them all?' because that would be obscene. Indeed, what question do I ask? 'Mirror, mirror, dare I go out today?' That seemed a good enough possibility. 'Mirror, mirror, what have you in store for me?'

This last question released a terrible memory in the analyst. A patient he liked very much had told him that in her early twenties she had gone to a guru in India, who had predicted: 'You will die at the age of fifty-four.' That was her mirror. She had dared to look into the future, and the mirror had spoken her fate. What was she to do with this? In fact, she kept it to herself, all her life, and when she reached fifty-five she breathed a sigh of relief. So, as we know, thought the analyst, mirrors don't always tell the truth. But what a horrible thing – what a horrible, horrible thing to carry that kind of prophecy in one's mind.

On a journey to America that year the analyst had discovered that there were clinics now that could scan the body – every cell of it – and not only declare the present state of affairs but foretell the future. In other words, we now had mirrors that could predict our death, although of course these clinics were asserting that this was simply a form of medical intervention.

He thought about this: intervention?

We really can intervene?

'Rubbish,' he said aloud, startling his wife, who was folding the laundry.

'What?' she said.

'What did I say?'

'You yelled out "rubbish". What did you mean?'

'Oh . . . bodies, and mirrors, and the whole damn mess of it all.' He stood up and walked out of the room to the loo.

His wife knew that he was lost in yet another of his passing depressed encounters, and that it was always best to leave him alone in these moments. They never lasted more than a few minutes and could usually be cured by tea or a walk around the block.

In a rare break with habit, the psychoanalyst left early for the office that morning, and on his way ran into local activist Francine Mestor, an acquaintance who rather frightened the analyst with her intensity. He noted that she bore a new object. 'What's with the whistle, Francine?'

She popped it into her mouth as if to blow it right then and there, and he immediately regretted his question. She was the sort of person, he thought, who could suddenly do things, and it was never quite clear to him what she might or might not do. Francine's whistle was bright red and swung from an elegant black leather necklace. One could not miss it. She asked if he had a moment and, as he did, they popped into Hippo for a coffee.

Francine told him the whole story. She had joined the Anti-Anti-Depressant League, or AADL. Any member of AADL would blow their whistle as loudly as possible upon hearing the word 'bipolar'; and as AADL was now increasing in numbers it was not uncommon to hear the piercing sound of whistles in the section of the city where most psychiatrists and GPs practised.

The psychoanalyst chided Francine for having kept this a secret. He said he had understood that she didn't believe in the life of the mind – the psychological mind, that is – but she quickly corrected him and told him that AADL had nothing whatsoever to do with the mind; it was a political and therapeutic recovery group from a form of addiction.

'Addiction to what?' asked the psychoanalyst.

'Addiction to depression. By extension, AADL is against anti-depressants, seen as so-called cures, because in fact they simply support the addiction. Some people can safely drink wine or spirits, others cannot – they suffer from alcoholism, which is a disease. Some people get depressed and it's simply part of their life, while others become addicted to depression, and it is this addiction to depression that we are against.'

'And the whistles?'

'We're whistle-blowers. Every time a shrink or doctor says "bipolar" we blow the fucking whistle on them because usually they're supporting the addiction to depression. It's a con, and the anti-depressants not only do not work but the very concept of them colludes with this addiction; and we're not standing for it any more.'

Francine's cappuccino and the psychoanalyst's espresso arrived, along with Gideon, the café owner, whose right it was to sit in on any interesting conversation he happened to hear. So now they were three. In fact a few seconds later they were five, as they were joined by Festor Bell, an optician, and Victoria Dink, a freelance journalist, much to Francine Mestor's pleasure.

The psychoanalyst brought everyone up to date and Victoria asked how the AADL meetings worked.

'Anyone can join,' explained Francine, 'if they're sponsored and they come along to a meeting, just like anyone entering any twelve-step programme.'

'So they have to fess up, is that it?' asked the optician.

'We invite them to make a statement, any statement they wish, and then we respond.'

'And if they use the word "bipolar"?' asked the analyst.

'Well you can imagine the sound of fifteen whistles going off at the same time.'

'But that sounds like terrorism,' said Gideon.

'Young man,' she said, glaring at him, '*depression* is terrorism. And we are counter-terrorists, and this is war.'

The psychoanalyst was rather pleased to hear someone with what seemed like an entirely different take on it to his own. 'Why is depression terrorism?' he asked.

'Because when people are diagnosed as' – she reached for her whistle and gently blew the word 'bipolar', a musical trick which the group found rather amazing – 'they are given a type of death sentence. It's like a diagnostic cancer and they live under the fear that if they don't immediately start taking anti-depressants and probably stay on them for life, they will be overcome by the Big D.'

'So what happens when they make their statement?' asked Victoria.

'Well, we listen, and if they say that they suffer from depression, we don't blow the whistle on them – that is reserved for the other word – but we give them the Long Face.'

'The Long Face?' asked Gideon.

'The Long Face,' repeated Francine, with relish.

She told the group that one of the AADL training programmes was a weekend theatre course in face-sculpting, which specialised in the imitation of different forms of depressed facial look. She rhetorically asked the group to recall the last time they had seen someone who looked depressed, and said that there was a kind of hang-dog look to the depressed person which AADL had termed the Long Face.

'You have no idea,' she continued, 'absolutely no idea of the devastating effect it has on the so-called depressed person to be given the Long Face. Imagine fifteen people suddenly hang-dogging on you. It's like looking in the mirror and the mirror collapsing into a kind of visual "yuck". It's very sobering.'

'But some people must run out of the room when this happens, surely?' asked Festor. Festor Bell was well known and successful as a local optician but he was a clearly depressed man who – rumour had it – looked into people's eyes because he found gazing into these gems, as he called them, a strange antidote to his own deadening mental life. He was obviously fascinated, if horrified, by Francine Mestor's lecture.

'No, very few people run. In fact, I myself have never seen it. Instead they usually smile in recognition and . . .'

'Then what?' asked Victoria.

'We give them the High Smile.'

Francine went on to tell them that part of the face-sculpting weekend was devoted to the High Smile, which was like a facial high-five. During this section of the course people learned what the AADL called the 'radiant beam' – a kind of shining light coming from the face that was found to be curative. She told them that there was a great literature on smiling. Scientists had found that there were well-known low-smile parts of the world (Buffalo, New York, for example) and they had discovered the ingredients of high-smile cultures (evident in, for example, employees at any of the Disneylands). The scientists in question then performed an experiment. They trained university undergraduates to enter the lowest of all recorded low-smile localities: a bar in Buffalo famous for its poetry readings, where no one had been seen to smile in fifteen years. They found that even relatively unattractive high-smilers could, with proper training, bring about a smile in the bar regulars, and that the vital ingredient was the 'radiant beam'. So AADL trained its group leaders to use this technique in first encounters, and lesser-grade 'beams' in the future course of the twelve-step programme.

The psychoanalyst asked Francine what the stages of the treatment were and, since he let her know he had only a few minutes, she picked up the pace. She told them that once a person confessed to being addicted to the term 'depression' and threw away their anti-depressants, they were given a red whistle. They were to report to their sponsor every day and they had to physically meet three times a week at first. The sponsor would listen out for signs of depression and if these were present, the sponsor would immediately confront the addict and it would constitute part of the week's report. That report also included the 'visuals' – which remained, she admitted, very controversial. The visuals consisted of photographs taken three times in the week that would then be kept in what was called, rather uncreatively, the photo album. The fifteen people attending the Saturday morning group would go through the photo album and rate the looks on the faces, using a scale of 1 to 100. A rating above 70 meant a person was depression-free. Below that it was graded from 'mildly addicted' to 'severely addicted'. It was controversial, she added, because 'pictures do not lie' and people could not get out of this by telling false stories: the evidence was right there in front of them.

The psychoanalyst excused himself from the conversation, left Hippo and walked to his office. Nearly. In fact, he landed on his favourite bench some hundred metres away. Another look at his watch told him he still had twenty minutes free – a result of having left early for work. He could genuinely thank his unconscious for telling him he had to leave, thus releasing him in good faith from Francine Mestor's company. Sitting on the bench, he could reflect on what AADL might or might not be. He thought it was rather ingenious to call certain depressions 'addictions', and he was more or less in agreement about anti-depressants. But he was troubled by the whole shame culture of the twelve-step programmes. Why did we have to declare ourselves ill in public? What was the point of this kind of self-disclosure? It seemed to him that this in itself was a form of madness, an ironic ally of the very thing AADL was opposing: the pharmaceutical industry and its take on the mind. The twelve-step programme was just a psychological analogue to Napalmtrek®, a kind of religious alternative that used the serotonin of shame as antidote to its designated enemy. It seemed to return adults to childhood – to a kind of playground culture of humiliation in which everyone had to confess to being a kid, always a kid, now and for ever. These simple tricks, these oddball meetings and their greetings, the whole idea of remaining 'an addict for ever': it all seemed to the psychoanalyst to be a kind of sleight of hand. The twelve-step programme offered a medically sanctioned leave of absence from reality, in perpetuity.

Yet maybe this was mental sour grapes on his part. After all, he mused, psychoanalysis was losing out to the self-help movement. Examination of the mind was really no longer of much interest to people. Indeed, he reckoned it had become in its own right a nominated illness. Some months previously he had attended a conference on ADD, Attention Deficit Disorder, fulfilling a requirement of his licensing board that he gain so many points each year by updating his expertise. In fact he was compelled to listen to what he thought of as mentally shallow idiots talking about a virtual explosion in the number of attention disorders affecting children, with, of course, the usual range of drugs being peddled. It was towards the end of the day, when he was tired, that Mavis Manhutten was brought on – no doubt it had been planned by the conference committee that they would save their big punch till last. Mavis Manhutten was a tough African-American psychologist, who told the congregation of about eighty therapists that there was now irrefutable evidence that ADD could be found in children of two or three, and that the only solution was early psychotropic intervention. To wait any longer, she said, was criminally negligent, and indeed Manhutten was proposing that all pre-schools should have mandatory psycho-diagnostic screenings so that any child found to have ADD could (and should) be put on medication immediately. She favoured something called AK47, an offshoot of Ritalin – of course, the drug's association with the well-known weapon was enjoyed to the full by manufacturers Guilded Lilly, who were vigorously promoting AK47 as the only way to 'shoot down' ADD. Manhutten argued that no parents could refuse their child's treatment, and she cited the case of Grosz vs The State Of Delaware, in which the Grosz family had tried to prevent the mandatory medication of their three-year-old son. The court found that in a case of this kind the child's right to treatment took priority over the parental right of choice, and in Manhutten's opinion this ruling was an appropriately ominous message to those who were dragging their feet in facing ADD. She then went on to present the 'case' of Freddy, who at three was found to have a hard time concentrating on his homework, was often distracted in the classroom, especially when there were girls present, and who would on occasion throw things at other children in his after-school playgroup. He had been put on AK47 and within four months his behaviour had changed dramatically. He could sit at his desk for up to forty-five minutes without moving, after which he had to take a 'micturation break', as AK47 intensified urination, and he was no longer distracted by the girls because AK47 had an 'appropriately depressing effect on the child's libido'.

Manhutten continued, listing the other changes in Freddy's behaviour, following which proceedings should have been brought to an end. Certainly the psychoanalyst intended to play no part in what was going on, but he made an unconscious slip by rolling his eyes to the ceiling. Later on, he could not even recall doing this – but Manhutten, who he knew absolutely had to be a paranoid personality from her stridency and militant presentation, saw his facial gesture. She stopped abruptly and said: 'I see that the gentleman' – she paused over this last word with clear sarcasm – 'in the fourth row has some doubts about what I am saying. May I ask your name, sir, and would you be kind enough to share your doubts with our group so that we might have an appropriate discussion?'

The psychoanalyst hated public speaking. He was no good at it. He never knew what he was going to say. These seemed to be the moments eagerly awaited by his unconscious – which was clearly stage-hungry – in which it could burst onto the scene with horrifying lines of logic and the occasional mortifying slip of the tongue. He was always amazed that others could apparently speak in public with no such worries and no signs of unconscious interference.

So he started off on the wrong foot by saying: 'Me?'

Mavis Manhutten sneered at him with victorious contempt – and roared with laughter when her weasel of a partner on the panel, Phillip Montrose, said, 'Maybe this good gentleman should try AK47: then he might be more attentive.'

That insult seemed to set something off in the psychoanalyst, and later he had to thank his unconscious for taking over in a rather eloquent way on this occasion. He said that his attention had not indeed wandered off – rather, he found Manhutten offensive and bullying. It was fair enough, he argued, to liken his state of mind to ADD, but might his symptom not inform the group of something about the children being discussed – whose childhood they were only too keen to rob, by numbing them through medication?

'Who has the attention deficit disorder?' he asked. 'The child, or you, or the parents?'

Without stopping, he went on to answer his own question. Since the mid-sixties it had been clear that although people might easily choose to have children, too many parents did not know what to do with them, so the children were bundled off to pre-pre-school, given homework, and taken care of afterwards by nannies or childminders. It seemed clear to him that those with the attention deficit disorders were actually the parents, plus the entire culture that supported this form of attack on childhood. What infuriated him, he added, was not only that parental culture was not prepared to take time with the child – to give the child the attention that he or she needed – but that these parents were *projecting* their own disorder into the child, both in deed and in name. He said he thought that this was a true crime, and that to cap this crime against future humanity by giving the children AK47 was akin to a nation being in the hands of some godforsaken dictator who tortured people, drove them to a state of anxiety, and then turned them into the walking dead by medicating them.

'Are you accusing me of being a dictator?' screamed Manhutten.

'You would be, I fear, if you could be – but actually I see you more as a kind of concentration camp leader, and by concentration I don't mean a camp that improves intellectual functioning. I'm here because you and your cohorts have shanghaied the licensing board and I'm forced to come and get these damn "target points" which, absurdly enough, are supposed to prove that I'm gaining in expertise.'

'I think this gentleman,' retorted Manhutten very slowly, 'shows us the kind of problem we face in the modern world.' Glancing at her clipboard, she went on: 'I can see that our sceptic is a psychoanalyst.' She paused and looked around the room. 'That's right, a psychoanalyst. For those of you who don't know what that is . . .' – her eyes gleamed as she surveyed the room a second time – '. . . a psychoanalyst is a follower of the late-nineteenth-century Sigmund Freud, who, as we know, is a completely discredited, unscientific thinker who managed for nearly fifty years to con the world into thinking we were guided by what he called the "unconscious". And we can see from the psychoanalyst's response today just how the few remaining members of this profession function. Set against all of our research we hear his armchair theory that those children who we are protecting through psychotropic intervention are instead, according to the psychoanalyst, victims of *perjection*.'

'That's "projection",' said the psychoanalyst, 'not "perjection" – which, incidentally, I've never heard of, but it sounds rather interesting to me.'

'Well *excuse* me,' Manhutten replied, 'for failing to recall the good psychoanalyst's *scientific term*. But where we have science behind us, where we have an entire international industry of psychopharmacology – based on biology, chemistry, neurology and psychology, and backed by every government in the Western world – the psychoanalyst merely has a *view.* Merely a view.'

Fortunately perhaps for the psychoanalyst, the clock struck five and the meeting was concluded. Depending on who one talked to, either he had won the debate or, as he heard from a cognitive psychologist through the grapevine, he had been 'fucked by Manhattan' – a mistake for being 'screwed by Manhutten', but what did it matter? Objectively, it was true that there was no scientific back-up to his theories. What did he know about ADD? All he knew was that each and every child with this tag who he had seen or supervised had been neglected by the mother or the father. From his point of view it was not a matter of blaming the parents, but of recognising that children needed to have their parents around. They needed the mother or the father at home when they returned from school, as they were vital characters in helping kids break down from the strains of reality. Going to school was tough, and kids needed to come home and regress a bit in order to go back out there the next day. It was no good if the parents weren't there, he thought, and it was a catastrophe if kids were given homework to do at the age of three or four when what they needed to do was play and forget about reality for a while. The world was unwittingly predisposing its entire population to a mordant after-effect: to the inevitability of depression following adolescence, when millions of people would feel some deep inner loss but not have a clue about its origins.

Why was he recollecting all of this while sitting on the bench, especially on a beautiful day? As he got up to walk the remaining distance to his office, he knew it had something to do with Francine Mestor's programme and the feeling he had that psychoanalysis was being pushed out of the cultural mix. But fortunately he had a new patient to see.

When the psychoanalyst greeted Kalid al Walid in the waiting room he saw a tall, very well dressed man of Middle Eastern appearance, with deep-set brown eyes and a slight tremble on his left hand. After Walid sat down, the analyst asked why he had come and Walid countered in a polite but quite determined way with a question of his own.

'You are a member of the Association for Confidentiality in Psychoanalysis, is that correct?'

'Yes,' replied the analyst, thinking to himself: oh no, not *another* paedophile.

'That means there are no circumstances under which you would report any person who comes to see you to the authorities, no matter what it was that they were talking to you about.'

'Yes, that's right.'

'That means also that if you were called upon by the authorities to discuss one of your patients, you would also refuse to do that, is that right?'

'Yes,' said the analyst.

'And you keep no notes, no record of your patients?'

'I keep a code for their names with telephone numbers and addresses, unless the person asks that even that not be kept.'

'I would want no record of my name, address or phone number please.'

'You seem very concerned about confidentiality,' said the analyst in a neutral but nonetheless rather pointed way.

'It is important for a person in my position to have this clear from the beginning, as I need help.'

'Help with . . . ?'

'Anxiety,' his new patient replied. 'As you can no doubt see, my left hand is trembling.'

'Yes, I see.'

'It is not neurobiological – I have been checked out. This is a problem that has arisen out of an anxiety related to a task, and I must master that anxiety if I am to carry out the task.'

'Perhaps the task raises the necessity of anxiety,' suggested the psychoanalyst.

'The task is high-risk. It involves lives and deaths, and I must be able to control my anxiety or I cannot fulfil the task.'

The psychoanalyst had only ever had a few out-of-body experiences. One had been while he was surfing, in his early twenties, on a day when the waves were huge. He had seen a monster set arriving from much further out than he was situated – the waves were at least twenty-two feet high – and as he swam out to 'meet' them it was as if he were suspended from his body and swimming in the air; as if his body could not believe where it was. His present experience with Walid was different, but it brought the surfing moment to mind by association. He felt a cold chill occupy his body and at the same time he felt unusually light-headed, as if Walid had refrigerated him and he had only a smidgen of oxygen left – hardly enough to think, much less talk.

The psychoanalyst tried to solve his dissociated state by clearing his throat, a technique that had worked before. Throat-clearing was a wonderful kind of self-help, as it suggested through sound that vocalisation was to follow shortly, even if the throat-clearer had absolutely no idea what to say. He often thought of it as a kind of somatic supplication to his unconscious, a way of saying: 'Well now, over to you, partner.' More often than not a clear comment would arrive out of his mental confusion, and he would be delivered once again by speech.

No such luck this time. When he attempted the throat-clearing, something rather awful happened instead. The psychoanalyst uttered what could really only be described as a scream. It was not a loud scream, more the kind of gagging sound produced by someone coming up from behind and grabbing him by the throat, though there was no one there except for Walid, who was sitting four feet in front of him.

'Are you all right?' asked Walid.

'Yes, I'm sorry: odd sound. I . . . uh . . .'

'Please. I think it is important once again to hear from you that nothing I say to you, under any circumstances, will leave this room. This is correct, is it not?'

The psychoanalyst gathered himself together and repeated that this was true: nothing would lead him to report a patient. He had joined ACIP, the Association for Confidentiality in Psychoanalysis, because paedophiles and others who needed therapy were unable to seek treatment from 'ordinary' therapists or analysts, as such clinicians had subscribed to the so-called reporting laws. Even though nothing frightened him more, the psychoanalyst was prepared to go to prison for contempt of court if necessary.

Walid's initial questions and the psychoanalyst's answers had taken up an unusually large part of the session, but Walid was clearly a man in a hurry. After establishing that he had another half-hour of the analyst's time, he explained that while he was training for his task a particular idea had crossed his mind which he thought prompted anxiety sufficient to make his hand tremble and to put completion of his task in jeopardy. The psychoanalyst asked what this idea was. After pausing and looking very clearly into the psychoanalyst's eyes, Kalid al Walid began to unbutton his shirt, to reveal beneath it what seemed to be a bright green undervest, which the psychoanalyst at first mistook for some kind of swimwear, until he saw the sight that had been in the public eye since the Catastrophe: the sight of a suicide bomber's vest.

'Why are you wearing this?' asked the analyst, without any thought behind the question.

'That should be obvious.'

'Obvious?'

'It *should* be perfectly obvious,' said Walid.

'It should be obvious that you are wearing a . . . a . . .'

'Martyr's vest.'

'It's for killing,' said the analyst.

'No, it is for justice. I am not here, however, to discuss politics with you. I have a task, an idea comes to my mind that interferes with my task, and I need your help with this idea.'

Stunned, as if paralysed by the sight of the vest, the psychoanalyst nonetheless asked after the idea.

'As I push this button,' said Walid, 'the following idea comes into my mind. The idea that interferes with my task is

82

the idea that the vest will not explode, because I have failed to charge it properly; and that I will not be a martyr but a laughing stock, and I see the family of my true love laughing and saying: "Walid always was a wanker." That idea is so strong that my hand shakes and so I must get rid of it.'

'What do you think of when you think of charging something properly?' asked the psychoanalyst.

'Doing it right,' replied Walid

'And what comes to mind about being a wanker?'

'Not doing something right.'

'So by not charging your vest right, do you not think it's a way of saying that you don't have what it takes, and that whatever your intention, you are, after all, just a wanker?'

Walid smiled knowingly, as if he were at last getting true help. The analyst looked at his watch, and feeling he could bear no more, decided to call a halt to the session. He apologised to Walid and told him that they would have to stop.

'But when do I get to see you again?' asked Walid. 'This is urgent.'

'I can see you next week, at the same time.'

'No. It has to be tomorrow.'

'But I have no time tomorrow.'

'I'm afraid you do.'

'I do?' asked the analyst.

'Between 12 and 1.30.'

'But that's my break.'

'You will be paid handsomely. Anyway, I do not wish to be discourteous, but we have no choice.' Walid then stood up, shook the psychoanalyst's hand, and walked out of the room.

It would be difficult to describe the psychoanalyst's state of mind, not least because it was by no means clear that he inhabited such a state. It was more as though he was dispersed along many lines of body-thought, disseminated through his physical self out into the object world like some kind of acid trip that connects self to objects. Some would say he was in a pocket psychosis, but this would not be exactly correct. It was not a psychosis of his own mental creation but a moment when psychosis occurs in the real, when reality breaks from itself, loses itself, and although the self does indeed lose its relation to reality, it is not up to the self to get it back; reality has to return to itself.

The analyst regained consciousness of himself, some minutes after Walid's departure, to find that he was lying on his couch – something he never did – looking up at the cornices on his ceiling. He was staring in particular at the eastern wing of the ceiling and a thought crossed his mind. The thought was actually a question: 'What?' The question returned at intervals of ten or fifteen seconds. This recurrence was only broken when the analyst suddenly – thoughtlessly – got off the couch, walked into his small kitchen, poured himself a large glass of water and drank it down very slowly and deliberately, as if he were filling something rather delicate. He then sat in his chair and stared at the fig tree in the corner of the room, in particular at the new leaves that were light green, so beautiful because they were set against the dark green of the older leaves. 'Ah, youth,' he thought; and it was this apparently innocent, indeed trivial idea, that snapped him out of his torpor.

'My God, what am I going to do?' he wondered, almost saying it aloud. He could section Kalid al Walid, as he was a

clear threat to himself and others, but that would violate
confidentiality because he would have to give a reason for
the section, and he could not do that. He could call a colleague
from ACIP but the idea of talking to anyone about what he
had just heard and seen made him ill. The sight of that vest
– and now he turned away from his green tree – that sickly
green vest which looked ribbed, surely because that was where
the explosive was to be . . . or, was it already there? Was this
man walking around the city already explosion-ready?

That could not be, the analyst thought. He was
practising, surely. Walid was trying to get accustomed to it
because the thought of his task was making him anxious and
he was attempting a cognitive therapy cure – a kind of
behavioural conditioning. The analyst could not get his mind
off the vest until he became aware of a specific aspect that
troubled him. He realised that the only terms under which
Walid's unbuttoning of his shirt would have been acceptable
would be if Walid had been Clark Kent turning into
Superman. The analyst realised that he must unconsciously
have been waiting to see the big S, but instead he saw the
garment representing what another psychoanalyst had called
the 'malignant transcendent'. Malignant transcendence was
the odious form of transcendence achieved by the serial killer,
who offered himself as a kind of helping angel to his victim-
to-be: eliciting trust, becoming like a God of sorts, and then
transforming himself into evil before the victim's eyes, prior
to killing him, and in this moment transcending the terms of
life and death.

Since the Catastrophe, however, the psychoanalyst had
thought that even the malignant transcendent had ceased to
exist, in that the categories of good and evil had been reversed.

Good people had been forced into evil action, while the victims of such evil action – who had been part of the structure of oppression and therefore could be seen as part of the Evil Empire – were now no longer evil because they were victims. The psychoanalyst believed that meaning itself had now left the world, so it did not matter whether good and evil were inverted because these terms no longer meant anything.

What was he to make of this man? Walid looked perfectly normal, the analyst thought. He looked decent and kind and good. And perhaps he was. In fact, the psychoanalyst was sure this was not a wicked man, but a vulnerable guy who was worried that he could not successfully blow himself and others up. He was trying to be responsible!

Without knowing quite why, the psychoanalyst ran down his stairs and out into the street in a kind of exhilarated mood. The idea that Walid was trying to be responsible and do the right thing just struck him as absolutely hilarious. He got to the bench, laughing, and said: 'I don't believe it. I just don't bloody believe it.' He rolled his head back and looked up at the sky through the outreaching arms of the giant plane tree.

'You don't believe what?' asked a voice. It was Fred Murk.

'Oh God, not you,' the analyst said. 'Not now.'

'That's a fine greeting, I must say!'

'Look, Murk – not now, please.'

Murk sat on the bench next to him. 'Do you know you were talking out loud?'

'I've no idea, and I really don't care.'

'Well surely it's not a very good thing for a psychoanalyst to do within a stone's throw of his office, especially after a patient has just left – the psychoanalyst almost crying and saying that he can't bloody believe it.'

'So be it,' the analyst said.

'Jesus, what *is* the matter with you? I don't think I have ever seen you like this. What's the problem – your last patient a terrorist or something?'

'What!'

'A terrorist?'

'What!'

'Jesus, you heard what I said,' replied Murk, who now turned to face the analyst directly. The analyst stared back, petrified, and the blood drained from Murk's face. 'Oh shit. I'm right – you've just seen a fucking terrorist, haven't you?'

'Shut the fuck up, Murk.'

'Oh my God.'

'I said shut up.'

'What are you going to do?'

'It's none of your business,' replied the analyst.

'What, it's none of my business that there's a terrorist in town? That's none of my business?'

'No, what I meant to say was: my patients are none of your business.'

'It's my business and everyone's business if you are seeing a terrorist.'

'Look, Murk, I mean that who I see is none of your business. I didn't say I was seeing a terrorist. I would never say something like that.'

'Well, I'm sorry, but you did say that.'

'What?'

'That is what you said.'

'I said nothing of the kind.'

'You did, when you told me to fuck off,' said Murk.
'You would never have talked to me like that unless I'd been
right. You would have given me one of your pious and well-
rehearsed microlectures about how your work is confidential;
but when I said "terrorist" I hit the nail on the head and you
have revealed all. I know you saw a terrorist: it showed in
your face and in your voice. The guy is all over you, inside
you, and spilling out of you right now as we speak. And what
are you going to do about it?'

'I'm going to give him your name, address and phone
number, and tell him that he should have you taken care of.'

'What?'

'You heard me,' said the analyst.

'You're shitting me.'

'No, I'm serious.'

'You're going to . . . he could . . . he would kill me.'

'That's the whole point.'

'You wouldn't do something like that. That would be
murder.'

'Well, Murk, right now I think it would actually give
me pleasure to throttle you myself, so—'

'You are kidding about all of this, aren't you?'

'About what?' the analyst asked.

'About telling him my name and giving him my
address.'

'I assure you, Murk, that *if* I were seeing a terrorist –
which is a big "if" – and if you dared speak this to anyone,
much less to the authorities, I would be obliged to tell this
supposed terrorist that there had been a breach of
confidentiality and to give him the name and address of the
person who was in possession of the breach.'

'What do you mean, "obliged"?'

'It's in the ACIP charter, under clause 9(b), which – if recollection serves me – says something like: "In the event that a third party breaches the confidential relation between the psychoanalyst and his patient, the psychoanalyst must immediately notify the analysand of this breach and supply the analysand with the name, phone number and address of the third party who was involved in the breach." Go look it up, Murk, but that's what I think it says.'

'But he would kill me.'

'Yes, I'm sure he would.'

'He would?'

'Well, I would if I were him.'

For the first time in the psychoanalyst's life-long relation to Murk he saw his comic friend not only stumped but completely silenced. Murk just stared at him, mouth slightly agape, a blood vessel in his neck pumping away like a manic oil line, hands on his knees with palms up and open: a really pathetic sight. And these two figures might have remained in that position for quite some time, were it not for the fact that the psychoanalyst had to leave to see another patient. He patted Murk on the shoulder and told him not to worry, that all Murk had to do was to keep this one thought to himself and he could sleep at night and not have to worry about having his head cut off before morning.

As the analyst walked to his office and climbed the stairs he could hardly believe what had just happened. How had Murk guessed? Yes, he knew all that stuff about unconscious communication and all that, but how did Murk know? Only a comic genius could see something like that, he reckoned. It had to have something to do with Murk's timing, with comic timing, that always seemed to see between the lines of human life – that managed to catch on the rim of experience some glint from the supposedly unknowable. Freud said of the 'joke work' that it was like the dreamwork, and the psychoanalyst thought to himself that Murk must have a special unconscious suited not only to joke work, but to seeing a joke as it was happening: to joke perception. The sight of the analyst talking to himself on the bench must have been a joke, and therefore it was perceivable to someone capable of joke work. To Murk's eye, the analyst must clearly have looked like someone who had just had the shit scared out of him, and his unconscious had simply said: 'He has seen a terrorist.' It was that simple.

Byron Mourncaster must have been talking for a good fifteen minutes before the analyst heard anything he said; but this would not have mattered to Mourncaster, who was only too pleased on this occasion to have all the airtime to himself.

'So you see,' he was saying, with almost a lilt to his voice, 'there is very little reason for me to go on. I went to my reunion and everyone there has gone on to do impressive things. My best friend is a successful doctor and my old girlfriend is chief hairstylist with Channel Ten. They look upon *me* as a success, too, but I know differently. Just below the surface I am this confused, chaotic guy – and if they could see that, people would be shocked. Just shocked.'

'I doubt it,' said the analyst.

'You doubt it?'

'Well, if they choose to be shocked then they have the same problem you have, and probably they do.'

'What are you talking about?'

'What *we* are talking about, Mr Mourncaster, is the difference between our outward appearance and our inner reality. Your friends and you all *look* quite complete, and no doubt were well decked out for the party, but no one's inner life has that kind of completeness to it. You might not like it, and indeed the disparity between how we appear on the outside and how we look in our internal worlds is sometimes depressing, but it's hardly worth killing yourself over – unless, that is, your greed for domination knows no bounds.'

'My greed for domination?' Mourncaster sounded surprised. 'Me, dominate?'

'Yes, domination. Or choose whatever word you like, but essentially you are depressed at this moment because you are insisting that your internal world should accord with an ideal self, that you should be able to get ordinary internal life – chaotic, messy, embarrassing as it is – into some kind of ideal representation. No one I know has ever been able to do that, although I expect the likes of Napoleon and others have tried quite hard to achieve such transformations.'

'But I really do feel depressed. I don't feel dominant.'

'Yes, you are depressed,' the analyst said, 'but that's because you are insisting on a transformation that is categorically impossible: we simply cannot get our internal world to accord with any kind of ideal. Your depression is like a kind of kid, sulking over not getting what he wants. You throw the threat of suicide around like some spoilt child who keeps announcing that he will take his marbles back if he isn't allowed to win every game.'

Of course, no sooner had the analyst said this than he regretted the way he had put it; but Mourncaster's reply was rather interesting: 'You've never spoken to me like this before.'

'No – that's true . . .' said the analyst, wondering what the hell he could do now.

'I must say, I think you are right. I do often feel like a spoilt child. I think if you had talked to me like this earlier it could have helped.'

After Mourncaster had departed, the analyst really was out of sorts. Sarcasm was the last thing an analyst was meant to deliver to a patient, and yet his cryptic metaphor seemed to have reached Mourncaster in a way never before accomplished. He recalled the example of a famous American psychoanalyst who had written that one interpretation – a joke – had transformed a chronic paranoid patient. The patient complained each day that she had to come for her sessions by subway and was pursued by pickpockets, perverts, rapists and murderers. And all for what? For a session with this obviously privileged being. 'I suppose you come to work by limousine,' she had said with withering contempt. When the analyst had replied that this was not actually the case, she asked how he *did* get to his consulting room. 'By subway,' he had said. Surprised by this, the patient had asked whether he was afraid of the criminals, perverts and murderers down there. 'Of course not,' he had replied, 'they're after you, not me.' The author claimed that this joke transformed the analysis, and although hardly a recipe for interventions in general, the analyst believed it stood on its own as a kind of truth. And perhaps what he took as an insult to Byron Mourncaster really did work for him that day (although, psychoanalysis being what it was, Mourncaster's next depression would probably be sourced from something else in him).

The analyst found himself amused by a daydream in which he was dancing along the streets of his village singing 'It's a depressing day, a great depressing day' in true celebration of the artistry of depression, of depression as *jouissance*. However, he was quite sure that this would prove Murk right, and that he would lose referrals.

He felt bad about scaring the hell out of Murk. He was even slightly worried that he might have meant what he said. It felt like it. Maybe he really had no choice but to tell Kalid al Walid that Murk had guessed he was a terrorist and . . . No. Rubbish. He would never have handed Murk over – that was ridiculous.

But this did not help the psychoanalyst with the gravest professional dilemma he had ever encountered in his life. Walking to his house, he wondered what on earth he was going to do about Walid. And, rather like some voice from God (in whom he did not believe) he heard the answer: 'You will have to kill him.'

'What?' the analyst heard himself say to this voice. 'Kill him?'

'Yes, the only way to stop him and to preserve confidentiality is to kill him.'

'With what?'

'That's your problem, you will have to figure it out. A kitchen knife, maybe. But you will have to kill him.'

Lost in these thoughts, the psychoanalyst did not notice that he had passed his house; indeed, he had walked on through the tangle of streets straight into the park. He walked and he thought. He thought yes, he probably had to do this, to kill a terrorist. That way he would of course be arrested for murder and put on trial, but surely they would discover (without him having to say it) what Walid was up to and that the analyst had acted in the only way he knew how, while preserving his allegiance to the ACIP. At first he imagined a calm and thoughtful judge, tall and handsome, who at the end of the trial would instruct the jury to bear in mind that this psychoanalyst was faced with the most horrific of moral dilemmas. The man had a terrorist in analysis and he could not violate his oath of confidence; so, faced with the option of allowing Walid to leave and blow up God-knows-who, he instead elected to take Walid's life in order to save the people of his city. The analyst imagined jurors in tears, some with hands folded in prayers of gratitude, as they went off to make their decision, before returning immediately to announce his innocence.

He was picturing this and many other things in a fast-moving Bartók-like opera of the imaginary when all of a sudden he realised it was getting dark and he was lost in the park. He knew the area well, very well indeed, but the city prided itself on the fact that this was its 'wild park': there were signs warning people not to enter it at night because of the danger of getting lost. He did know to some extent where he was, however, because after a short time he found that he had walked into the Maze. The Maze was the only part of the park – other than the ponds – that was ordered. It was composed of thick, impenetrable holly hedges some twelve feet high, and during the day the park attendants, who knew the pattern of the Maze, regularly rescued scores of people who could not find their way out.

The analyst thought of calling his wife, who could alert the police, who in turn could contact the park authorities. He reached for his mobile phone, but was frustrated to find that there was no signal. He told himself that he should remain calm, reminding himself that every day lots of people did find their way out of the Maze. So he thought that perhaps he should just retrace his steps. He walked back and came to a T-junction where he thought he had turned right, so now he turned left, and at each succeeding junction he made a similar decision. But after an hour of this his walking pace slowed and his heart rate increased, while memories of his utter hopelessness at games of almost any kind began to seep into his mind. He remembered visiting his mother in a nursing home, when he had been asked by the nurse if he would kindly play draughts with her. At first he couldn't remember how to play; then when he did finally recall the basics, he was humiliated by the fact that even though his mother suffered from dementia, she consistently beat him.

No, the sad fact of the psychoanalyst's life, especially in such a moment as this, was that he lacked the imagination to play games of this kind. To enter a maze required a belief in a certain kind of intelligence and the psychoanalyst was not in touch with that type of unconscious knowledge. He did not give up, however, and continued walking; but he knew now that if he happened upon the exit to the Maze it would be pure chance. He stopped briefly to look at his watch and he was shocked to see it was nine o'clock. He had been walking for at least two hours, and now he sat down. He was rather seriously worried. At worst, this could mean spending a night in the Maze, and he was concerned about hypothermia and dehydration. As he often got chest infections, he knew he was going to pay for this. He got up again and for a while he walked in a circle, whispering out loud: 'Oh God, oh God, oh God.' Within the Maze he was so cut off from the world that he could not even hear the sound of night birds. It was an eerie quiet.

'Hello.'

The psychoanalyst froze. He was utterly terrified. He did not know what to do – what *could* one do in such a situation? A voice had said hello, but he could see nothing.

He replied tentatively: 'Uh, hello.'

'Are you lost?' asked the voice.

'I'm afraid I am,' said the psychoanalyst.

'I thought so.'

'Would you mind . . . I can't see where you are,' said the psychoanalyst.

'Yes, I am out of your sight.'

'It would help me if you would be kind enough to appear, because this is all so very unusual for me.'

'I appreciate that,' said the voice, 'but I prefer to remain invisible.'

'You do?' asked the analyst, who was still rooted to the same spot and terrified of looking around.

'What do you think of me?' asked the voice.

'What do I think of you?' echoed the analyst.

'Yes, what do you think of me?'

'I'm not sure I know what to think.'

'But you are thinking something, aren't you?'

'Yes, well,' said the analyst, 'I'm thinking . . . actually, to be honest, I'm more than a bit afraid.'

'Afraid of me?' asked the voice.

'Well, I'm not sure if it's you I'm afraid of, or the circumstances, or the fact that I can hear you but not see you.'

'I notice you have not looked around.'

'Yes, I think I'm rather terrified, to be honest.'

'That's a great shame,' said the voice.

'But understandable, don't you think?'

'Well, I am not you. It depends on who we are, this sort of experience. Tell me, what do you do?'

'I'm a psychoanalyst.'

'Freudian or Jungian?'

The psychoanalyst felt he was now in a terrible position. There was something about the tone of this voice that was almost divine, carrying a kind of sonic serenity, and he knew he should not lie. He reckoned that the whole experience seemed far more Jungian than Freudian and, moreover, that if the voice wanted such an immediate clarification, it must be a Jungian voice speaking and not a Freudian one. As the analyst hesitated, the voice spoke again:

'You're Freudian.'

'How could you tell?'

'Because you hesitated in the Freudian manner, not the Jungian,' said the voice.

'We hesitate differently?'

'Yes, Freudians refuse to speak and Jungians don't know what to say. I think you refused to speak, so I knew you were a Freudian.'

'I promise you,' said the analyst, 'I am not one of *those* Freudians.'

'So *you* say.'

'Are you going to help me get out of here?'

'Yes,' replied the voice.

'Oh, thank you very much. I must say, I really do need help.'

'Yes, I can see that,' the voice continued. 'But before I help you out of the Maze I have one or two questions.'

'Okay.'

'What do you think I am?'

'I'm sorry?'

'What do you think I am?' repeated the voice.

'I'm afraid I don't quite know how to answer this.'

'Well, what do you think I'm doing here?'

The analyst was well and truly stumped. Of course, it was very odd to come across a disembodied voice and he had never actually asked himself what this voice was doing in the Maze. Perhaps the absence of such curiosity on his part was to do with the overall traumatic nature of this experience.

'I'm surprised that I haven't asked that,' the analyst admitted.

'Well, think then. What would a person be doing out here at this time of night, in the Maze, and out of sight?'

'Well . . . I don't know exactly. I suppose you are . . . looking for privacy . . . or maybe you like the Maze by night?'

'It is pleasurable,' said the voice.

'So . . . that being the case . . . I suppose you are enjoying yourself.'

'What do you think of me sexually?'

'I beg your pardon?'

'What do you think of me as a sexual being?'

'Gosh, I've no idea,' said the analyst.

'Are you sure you're a Freudian?'

'Yes.'

'So, you're in a Maze . . . lost in one. It is now 9.15 p.m. and you hear a voice, a man's voice, call to you, and I have asked you what you think I am, and we have established that I find it enjoyable to be here. I am sure you realise that I can't help you out of the Maze unless you are perfectly honest with me . . .'

'Oh, I know that, I can feel that for sure.'

'So, I want to ask you . . . and think about this . . . what am I?'

Of course, the psychoanalyst would not ordinarily have been so stupid, but it had been a hell of a day, and he was genuinely traumatised and unable to think clearly. However, at last it struck him that of course the voice was that of a homosexual. So.

'You're homosexual.'

'You can say "gay" if you like.'

'Okay, gay,' said the psychoanalyst, although he hated that word for a number of reasons, not least because he did not think homosexuals were by and large all that happy. He knew that he suffered from a kind of residual homophobia, just as he was also a racist of sorts, exhibited class prejudice, and harboured all kinds of ethnic phobias – all the stuff that one had to discover about oneself if one wanted to become a Freudian: a terrible, gruelling rite of passage.

'What do you think of gay people?' asked the voice.

'Fine, in my view. I think, fine.'

'You told me you would tell me the truth.'

'Yes,' said the analyst.

'I think you're lying.'

'That's true. I am lying a bit.'

'What do you really think?'

'I think conflicting things,' said the analyst. 'I do confess to thinking at times that you . . . I mean gay people . . .'

'You can say "you" – I don't mind.'

'Well, I think that you suffer because I think you lose out by not being able to love a woman, to enter a woman with pleasure, because I think vaginas are wonderful.'

'I'm sure that is true, but why are they wonderful?'

'Because to enter a woman is to return to our origins, to return to where we came from, both personally – in that we are born from women – and phylogenetically, because the womb is the lost sea. We get to return to that ocean when we make love and I think it's tragic that you cannot do this. I don't think the anus is really an alternative, even though—'

'It really is quite exciting in its own way,' said the voice.

'I'm sure that must be true.'

'And your dreams,' asked the voice, 'your homosexual dreams?'

'I do have them from time to time.'

'And?'

'Well, I'm always horrified; especially if I have enjoyed them.'

'So you too are missing out on something.'

'Not something I wish to have anything to do with consciously.'

'And you, a psychoanalyst. Naughty, naughty! Why *do* you think you wandered into the park – indeed, into the Maze – at night?'

'Because,' said the analyst, 'I am looking for the solution to a terrible problem.'

'That only another man could solve.'

'I think you're right in one very convincing way: I do think I wandered in here to find God the Father, and it's a strange thing to say, as I do not believe in God.'

There was a momentary pause before the voice spoke again.

'Do you see the big oak tree in the distance?'

'Yes, just about,' said the analyst.

'Okay, now walk towards it and turn left at the first two junctions, then right at the next three, then left at the next two, and in ten minutes you'll be free.'

'Left at the first two, right at the next three, left at the two after that . . .'

'Then you will be at the oak tree. When you get to the tree, turn right, keep walking, and you will come to the Vale of Tears and there you will see your first street lamp. Goodnight.'

'Goodnight,' said the analyst; and he set off on his journey.

4

Terrorising terrorism

The psychoanalyst did not sleep well that night. He was haunted by images that never quite became dreams: the man revealing his green vest; the Maze and the voice; the oak tree, which seemed comforting but appeared and reappeared in his mind so many times that it began to wear him out. His wife had of course been very worried about his disappearance, so she had called the police – but he had got home just as they were ringing his front doorbell, at which point he explained that he had been out drinking and had not called the wife.

His wife could tell, however, that he was keeping something from her, but as he was being so evasive she reckoned he must have just had a particularly bad day. Sometimes she would go out looking for him when he did not return within an hour of his expected arrival, and she would always go first to the bench near his office, where she often found him just staring into the distance, arms stretched along the back of the bench. He was always pleased to see her, and she never scolded him because she knew that he was, as their children put it, just 'chilling', and that he needed to do what he was doing. William Glastonbury had once explained that her husband was simply 'emptying himself of the projections', and this made a certain sense – she often wondered how he could take so many stories, day after day. On one occasion she had asked him if that was in fact what he was doing, but he had said no – to his knowledge, he just loved sitting on that bench, watching people pass by, and he needed to be outside for a period of time. Unlike Glastonbury, who seemed to eat, breathe and sleep psychoanalysis, and was always talking in analytical terms, she never heard her husband use psychoanalytical language. He seemed to be against the use of psychoanalysis outside the consulting room.

The psychoanalyst hated disruptions to his routine, and he was meant to meet up with Westin Moorgate in the morning; but he called the journalist first thing and said that something had come up. Westin would of course have been horrified to learn what the psychoanalyst was doing: examining the knives in his kitchen because he imagined he was going to have to kill a patient that day.

His wife asked him what he was up to and he said that he was looking for a good knife, about five inches long and quite strong. She asked him whatever for, and he explained that he had a package at work that he had not been able to open.

So the psychoanalyst walked out into the street, half an hour before he usually would, carrying a knife inside his jacket, every so often feeling its blade thud against his chest. He pulled out his mobile phone, called the two patients he was meant to see before Walid, and left messages cancelling their sessions. He did not, however, cancel the patients after Walid – but this escaped his attention at the time. He walked past the shops on the High Street (most of which he loved to frequent, even if he had little reason to do so), and when passing a Moroccan restaurant called Zabar, it occurred to him that he was about to murder a person of the Islamic faith.

How could a person of faith kill people? He knew why he must kill Walid, he thought, but how could a Walid plan to blow up innocent people? He very quickly replied to himself that of course, they were at war: if Superpower had in effect declared war on Islam then of course Muslims around the world felt they had no choice but to fight. That they fought in the way they did was not surprising – in fact, he thought, it was rather like the way colonial Americans fought the British in the beginning: by cheating. While the British marched up and down New England in formation, the Americans would be hiding behind barns, trees and rocks, taking pot-shots at them. The British would drop their first line of troops down into firing position, from where they would offload a volley, to be replaced by the next line that marched forward – but even though the British tried 'shock and awe' against the Americans, it didn't work because the Americans, 'cowards and yellow-bellies' that they were, never came out to fight.

So he could hardly ask why Kalid al Walid was going to do what he intended to do. That would be absurd.

When noon came – after he had passed several nervous hours in his office, thinking about the situation he found himself in – the analyst saw the same tall figure: well dressed, eyes even more deeply set, and if anything, rather serene. Walid held out his hand and the psychoanalyst could see that he was not trembling. He was smiling.

'You are a very good psychoanalyst, I think.'

'Well . . .'

'No, I think so,' said Walid. 'I think very good.' He pulled out a white envelope and handed it to the analyst. 'Here you will find that there is more than enough compensation for your efforts.'

'Well . . . I don't think I can . . .'

'Oh, I am sorry, you must. This is more than just a matter of honour. Payment, as you know, cements our professional relation and so you are bound to fulfil your contract.'

'Yes, I see,' said the psychoanalyst.

As Walid continued speaking, the analyst reached into his left pocket and felt the knife. He gazed at the sweet-looking person across from him and knew that in a matter of minutes he would have to kill him. He had decided that he would tell Walid he had to close the blinds a bit and, walking past him, he would take out the knife and cut his jugular vein. That morning the analyst had actually practised the manoeuvre in his study, by setting up his globe of the world on top of a filing cabinet that was approximately the height of the seated Walid. Unfortunately he had destroyed a large part of the world in the process, but . . .

'So, your symptom is gone?' the analyst asked, trying to kill time.

'Yes, completely.'

'So, the idea of your not charging the vest properly and your wife's family laughing at you and calling you a wanker, this idea is gone, is it?'

'Not gone,' said Walid, 'but thanks to your good works yesterday, I know it simply means they think I am not capable of being potent, that it has nothing to do with whether I can pack the explosives – I know I can – and so, as you can see, I no longer have the shakes and I am absolutely confident.'

'Um. Tell me,' said the analyst, with no idea of what he was saying, 'when you imagined the family laughing at you, how many of them were there?'

'How many?'

'Yes. Was it, or is it, a big family or a small family?'

'It is five, not including my wife. Her father, mother, two brothers, and her older sister.'

'So it's not such a big family.'

'No, not really.'

'Have you ever thought about that?' asked the analyst, absolutely unclear about what this might mean.

'No – I, I . . .' Walid seemed thrown by the analyst's question, even slightly irritated. 'Is there some reason why this is important?'

'Well, of the members of the family who are laughing at you and calling you a wanker, who is it that is actually saying this?'

Walid paused for a while, eyes furrowing, concentrating. 'Well, I think it is the father who says this. Yes, it's the father saying this.'

'I see,' said the analyst. 'And when you imagine this, what time of day does it occur?'

'What time of day?'

'Yes – for example, could it be about half-past one, or two in the afternoon, while all of you are at the table, eating outside in the sun?'

'Yes . . . this is possible,' said Walid slowly.

'And could it be that your image is based on an experience of actually being laughed at by your wife's father – when he leant back and roared with laughter?'

'Yes, I think so,' replied Walid, now looking somewhat transfixed.

'Did you see his teeth?'

'His teeth?'

'Yes, did you see his teeth?' repeated the analyst.

'Yes, I did see his teeth.'

'I see. And he has gold fillings, yes?'

'How do you know that?'

'Don't worry,' said the psychoanalyst, now completely baffled by where his unconscious was taking him and what it was up to. 'Were there two gold fillings?'

'Yes. At least.'

'And when he leant back and laughed at you, did the sunlight catch one of the gold fillings, almost blinding you for that moment? And as this happened, did you turn to see his wife, your mother-in-law, and did you find that she was not only laughing, but heaving, and that as she is very heavy, her body shook with waves and waves of flesh rolling over her?'

'Yes!' said Walid, now gripping his chair with both hands, his knuckles white.

'Did the waves roll off her body into the ground, gathering Mother Earth's garments – leaves, grass, rock – and did they fragment and gather speed, and were they radiated by her husband's gold?'

Walid stared.

'Did you cry out and wander after these fragments, begging that your dignity be returned, and did Allah silence your voice and end the sound of our Mother Earth, so that you could not hear and you were without the brotherhood of birdsong?'

Walid's eyes began to glaze.

'And when you looked at her two sons, were they smirking but looking down at their shoes?'

'Not even looking at me.'

'That's right, not even looking at you. But worse than that: looking at their shoes, a sign of humiliation – a shoe is better looked upon than you.'

Walid was silent.

'And did you then look at your sister-in-law, and was she snorting with laughter, spuming snot from her nose, and did it actually spray your body?'

He nodded.

'And did it not seem that you were then made into the sign of the donkey, the mule of the group, simply there to be the spittle of laughter? And when you thought this, did you not think that your wife's family was a single beast, a kind of evil-tentacled Shaytan that was seeking to consume you and destroy your name? And did you not then look at your wife, whose support of course you needed, and did she not look . . . well . . . it is hard to capture the expression on her face . . . but did she not look upon you as if you were . . .'

'A wanker,' said Walid.

'A wanker. A pathetic wanker. An honourable man reduced by Superpower to this horrible position of being just a wanker. An oil wanker with no oil, a tanker with no spumen, a man with no woman, a son with no father?'

The psychoanalyst was no nearer to knowing what any of this meant, but he continued anyway.

'Because it's not just Superpower you want to blow up, it's your father-in-law, the man with the golden teeth, the man with the wife who rolls her body in fat laughter, the man whose sons look at you and see a shoe, the man whose wife thinks he is a wanker. It is that man that you want to blow up, and your hand trembles because, while you would like to sacrifice your life to blowing up Superpower, you cannot live twice and you actually want to blow up—'

'He stole my honour . . . I must prove . . . him wrong.'

'You can't, because you will fail. You will open his huge mouth again, the gold teeth will shine on the newspaper reporting your failure, the family will roll with fat humour and your name will be in shame for ever. The balls of fat that roll from their bodies will cascade down the hill of your village, each ball stopping in its fated place, to give root one year later to a special kind of pomegranate tree that every twenty-eight days will bear fruit that will explode blood-soaked seeds along a now infamous road, the road named after your dishonour. And their explosions will summon the yellow-winged bats that come out at night and these bats will catch the seeds and disseminate them across the land, and when the seeds hit the ground they will turn into miniature portraits of you, bearing a text stating that you were a wanker. And children will long to acquire these miniatures, they will compete for them with one another, and families will hang them on their walls, as your sign of shame is their mark of honour, and there will be festivals across the land every five years – special Wanker Walid festivals when families compare their portraits, as there are no two that are the same, and each festival will honour one family by giving them the golden tooth, a special replica of the tooth of Walid the Wanker's father-in-law, the tooth that drove the Wanker away. And then your village, cursed and deserted for years, will undergo a strange metamorphosis. The houses will eventually transform into shoes: they will turn into shoe-houses. It is Barzak. And then this village, which has been empty for so long, will receive its visitors, strange people who come walking down the pomegranate lane and call this place Paradise, and they will have been the suicide bombers who have been on a very strange journey . . .'

This is only a portion of what the psychoanalyst said. He became so lost in his narrative that he completely forgot about Walid. He even got up and walked about the room, lay down on his couch for a moment, and looked out the window. Then suddenly, as if snapped out of a trance, he stopped talking and walked briskly towards Walid, before sitting back down in his chair.

Walid was staring straight ahead and appeared not to be breathing. At first the psychoanalyst could not make sense of this paralysis until an idea crossed his mind. Christ, he thought, I've hypnotised him. The analyst was all the more amazed because not only had he never been trained in hypnosis, he actually did not believe in it – but sure enough, Walid was in a hypnotic trance. Fortunately the analyst realised this in good time. He said that after he counted to three, Walid was to leave the premises immediately, without speaking, and to forget the psychoanalyst for ever. He was to walk directly to the local police station on Lahr Road, go up to the desk sergeant, and say: 'Please do not harm me. I was a terrorist, I am wearing the green suicide vest, and I would like you to kindly remove it from me.' Walid was then to give up all idea and memory of being a terrorist for the rest of his life.

With bated breath the psychoanalyst counted to three. As if by magic – and, by God, that is what it looked like to him – Walid got up and walked calmly down the stairs.

The analyst was stunned. Events had moved so fast. He had no idea why he had done what he did, but as he sat in his chair it occurred to him that, of course, he had tried to make his patient ill. He had not knowingly embarked on this course of action: his conscious intent had been to kill the patient, not to commit mental abuse. But he was now faced with an ethical dilemma. Wasn't there a passage in the United Psychoanalytical Society's Code of Ethics that said it was unethical for a psychoanalyst to drive a patient mad? He had forgotten to tell the patient to forget the legend of Walid the Wanker – and furthermore he had practised hypnosis without a licence. He thought for a moment and wandered out of the consulting room into his office, where he picked up the UPS Code of Ethics and flipped through it, but found nothing about it being unethical for a psychoanalyst to drive a patient crazy.

And then he breathed a sigh of relief. In fact, he thought, many of his colleagues regularly drove their patients mad. What an irony that something that had bothered him all his life should now prove to be such a solace. Thank God for his colleagues who thought their patients were evil and who needed to show them how even the most apparently innocent communication was in fact a thinly veiled attack upon the psychoanalyst. Thank God for the fact that they had turned relatively troubled people into deeply disturbed and depressed souls, presided over by omniscient paranoid analyst gods who read them their unconscious intent day after day after day. The psychoanalyst had indeed driven Walid into a form of mental illness, and had in fact engendered a psychotic phantasy of his own shame in the eyes of his father-in-law, which really was horrible. But, on the other hand, he had saved lives.

After the dramas of these last hours, the psychoanalyst found himself strangely alone and depressed. Fortunately he had the good sense to cancel the day's remaining patients, as he was sure he would be unable to provide an adequate psychoanalytic ear. Sometimes when he felt depressed he would order himself to do something – to go for a walk, or listen to music, or telephone a friend. The inner voice that gave these directives had a quiet and reassuring sincerity to it; but today it remained silent, even though he asked out loud: 'What should I do?' When there was no answer he went to his small bathroom, where he washed his face several times, as if cleansing himself of the traumas he had experienced. He returned to his analytical chair, behind his couch, and sat there for about ten minutes, but eventually it struck him as absurd – this position was for the psychoanalytic task; not a place to hang about.

He did wonder, however, about his own depression. Could he claim that it really had to do with a kind of post-traumatic let-down? He didn't think so. Could he link his affect to anything in particular? As always, when he asked a specific question of his unconscious, he received a specific reply – though he was often disappointed by what he heard. Today he heard: 'You are depressed because your profession sucks.' It could, he thought, have been formulated more eloquently than that, but who was he to tell his unconscious it should find different words? Ask a question of this oracular part of the self and you get what you get.

So why did his profession suck?

Well, for one, the thought *thought*, it didn't exist. Or, the way it did exist was so full of fault lines that it was like being a member of some Mafia who had not found a way to gain real power and money, and were therefore left to bully one another for lack of anything else to do. He had never met a meaner, nastier, more small-minded group of people in his whole life. Actually, many analysts left to themselves were quite nice – it was what psychoanalysis did to them *as a group* that was so horrifying.

His mind wandered to the latest theoretical orientation that had taken America by storm: 'agent theory'. Agent theory, or 'agentalism', was advocated by 'agentalists', who argued that psychoanalysis was essentially about agency – but it suffered from conflicting theories about this. Of course, there was unconscious agency, but there were several differing *types*, so agentalists had written books sorting out this tangle of competing theories. Then, of course, there was an individual type of agency specific to each diagnostic category, and these also needed sorting out.

Apparently a group of ten people in New York had met over dinner one evening and decided that they should start a psychoanalytical movement. They figured out that it was really quite easy to do and was a good way to substantially increase their incomes. First they had to come up with a gimmicky name that was sufficiently generic to enable them to co-opt all other schools of analysis, and thus rewrite psychoanalysis in its entirety. It took a while, but as soon as

113

the concept of 'agency' came up, it practically rang its own bell.

Then the group did the next logical thing, which was to create a journal called *Agency*. They invited thirty eminent people – who knew next to nothing about the journal but would never decline any invitation of this kind to join a Board of Readers – and instantly they had an impressive list of supporters. Each member of the group then wrote a chapter in the seminal book *On Agency Theory*, which was to be a kind of compendium of agency thought but set out in such simple language that any idiot could understand it. This tome consisted of some six hundred pages, which made it look very comprehensive. (Psychoanalysts, who did not read much these days, were impressed when books were thick, as this clearly indicated the presence of seriousness of thought and weighty ideas.) There was a chapter on Freud's theory of agency, on Klein, Winnicott, Bion, Kohut, and all the other major thinkers, indicating their respective theories of agency and making it possible for the reader to digest these writers in alarmingly simple terms.

Alarming perhaps to those who were not agentalists – but after all, who could *not* subscribe to agentalism? The Gang of Ten, as the original editorial board of *Agency* called themselves, then invited 'select' people in the major cities of the USA to join them as editorial advisors and to hold the first agentalist congress. These 'point people', as the gang described them, were in turn to invite colleagues in their respective areas to hold weekly meetings and to invite members of the original gang to come and give lectures on such important topics as 'Gender and Agency', or 'Instincts and their Agents', or 'Compliance as Agency'.

Before the first year was over, they counted a solid three hundred signed-up agentalists in the USA, while the Gang of Ten had all gone on to edit different volumes on their theory and got others to do the same. Of course, no movement could survive unless it found enemies – this was vital to their momentum, because if they had not been opposed and people had simply shrugged their shoulders then nothing would have happened. So when the Steering Committee met and they asked who among the eminent analysts in the country was not 'on board', it was not difficult to find fifteen or so people who could then be 'blacklisted'. Not only were they not invited to any of the conferences, but their names would be dropped at crucial moments when recruits asked the logical question: 'Anyone have any difficulty with agency theory?' It was absolutely essential to zing out a few names so that the recruits could feel the rush of opposition from these otherwise well-respected figures, whose portraits were now hanging in the Hall of Shame of Agentalism.

The psychoanalyst often thanked his stars that he was a comparative unknown in his field. He hated research, found writing almost impossible, and loathed public speaking. One of his colleagues, Vitale Rampster, had fallen foul of the agentalist movement because he had turned down their invitation to be on the editorial board of *Agency*: this was enough to alert the Gang of Ten that he was a potential troublemaker. There was in fact no cause for alarm, since having Rampster as a nominal foe was great news for the movement – although Rampster was none too happy with the many moves made against his public persona. But as the psychoanalyst had told him: 'Well, Vitale, you took it on, and that's the nature of the beast.'

The psychoanalyst nonetheless felt a bit of a nerd, as he knew he lacked the courage necessary to stand up to the agentalists. He was as troubled as Rampster by the undeniable fact that fascist movements occupied psychoanalysis, just as they did many other groups in society. Look at the 'here and now transference interpretations', he thought. How much sicker could things get? It was the psychoanalyst who was the paranoid – the poor sod of a patient had to listen to this narcissistic monster referring every detail of the patient's life to the analyst, and not only as content but as action. It was as if the patient was seen as constantly trying to get one over on the analyst.

So was the psychoanalyst depressed by issues within his profession? He thought for a moment and said to himself that this seemed a bit too convenient. And like a weight announcing itself in his stomach, he knew that however troubling all this was, he was actually avoiding something much closer to home. His term on his society's Ethics Committee was at last – after four years – coming to a close, and in these four years his life had changed, he believed, beyond all measure. He had originally looked forward to serving because he reckoned that it was a forum where important ethical issues would be debated. He liked the seven other people on the Committee, especially the Chair, Winifred Slinder, who seemed beautiful, charming and, he was sure, full of integrity. For a while the matters that came before the Committee seemed routine enough: a patient complaining about an analyst's fees; an analyst complaining about the fact that a colleague had called him a shit in a scientific meeting; a member of the public hearing that a long since deceased analyst had fucked two of his patients.

The Committee dealt well with these matters and the psychoanalyst always looked forward to the meeting.

That was until a colleague, Cloggs, brought a complaint – not a serious one, but a complaint nonetheless – against another colleague, Bloggs. The psychoanalyst was aware that all but two of the members sitting on the Committee were much too involved with Bloggs and should not be hearing the case. One member shared a consulting room with Bloggs; another was married to Bloggs's sister; another was analysing Bloggs's brother; and another was the spouse of Bloggs's accountant. One was the editor of Bloggs's latest book – and finally, as if that were not bad enough, Winifred Slinder was to be the discussant at its celebration launch. The psychoanalyst fully expected that one by one his colleagues would excuse themselves from hearing the case, given these clear conflicts of interest. But no, Slinder went right into the matter and asked the members what they thought. All considered that the complaint brought by Cloggs was serious, but really not serious enough: it was more of a 'spat' than a matter of ethics. Instead of objecting to the situation and pointing out that he thought the members should not be hearing this case, and that they should ask for assistance from former Committee members, the psychoanalyst said nothing. Matters worsened when Cloggs complained about the very thing that was bothering the psychoanalyst, but Slinder said: 'Now we have this new complaint from Cloggs, so does anyone here agree with him that we are not capable of being objective?' Of course, everyone assured her they could be objective. As Cloggs continued to press for a fair hearing, Slinder eventually arranged for two kinds of meeting: one in which they did not discuss Cloggs vs Bloggs, and another in which they did. That way, Cloggs should have been assured of receiving an impartial hearing. The problem was, however, that the entire Committee was in fact present all the time, and actively involved in discussing the issue until Slinder announced: 'Now we are having our official meeting' – at which point only she, the psychoanalyst and the one other member who did not know Bloggs so well would talk about what to do.

In his daydreams the psychoanalyst was often a hero. He would imagine a child falling into a fast-moving river and he would jump in, swimming below the surface of the water to rescue the child, who was near death. He would struggle with the child back to the shore, where he would collapse while receiving the praise of all those who witnessed his fearless action. If he had enough time for this daydream, he might even be interviewed by the papers, or perhaps it had all been captured by a passing news crew. The psychoanalyst would be embarrassed to have to enumerate the number of heroic scenes he provided for himself during an ordinary day.

But now he had another kind of daydream, that began as a sickening feeling. The sickening feeling was that he had taken part in a corrupt Ethics Committee, that even though he was well thought of and considered a person of integrity, he had in fact colluded with something he knew to be a terrible violation of Cloggs's rights. He knew that Bloggs was by far the more influential figure in the Society and this was one of the reasons that Slinder – who saw Bloggs as a key power-broker – did not want to be on the wrong side of him. So the analyst grasped the reasons why this happened. But it was not just that he was troubled by analytical movements or bad practice; this had to do with his own failure of character. It moved into daydream when he imagined a day in the future when a White Paper might be written on his Society, in which the work of the Ethics Committee would be scrutinised and it would be found that he had taken part in an unethical action.

That was why some months ago the psychoanalyst had travelled all the way to Greece to meet with the Chair of Ethics of the international organisation of which his society was a constituent member: the Universal Psychoanalytical Association. He had asked for this meeting in the strictest confidence because he thought he had been part of a serious miscarriage of justice and he wanted advice. Dr Paris Annoulis was by far the most eminent ethicist in the psychoanalytical world, and as Chair of the UPA's Ethics Committee he was rather like a god – the analyst found it fitting that he was Greek. Annoulis told the psychoanalyst to send him in advance as much detail as he could, in order that he could familiarise himself with the situation, so the psychoanalyst wrote a small monograph detailing what had happened. When they met in Athens Annoulis said: 'Now, I want you to know that we have the entire afternoon – three hours – so take your time.' The psychoanalyst nearly broke down in tears because he was so deeply grateful that Dr Paris Annoulis was taking him seriously.

It had taken the analyst almost two hours to describe his situation, with Annoulis nodding and occasionally umming, and the psychoanalyst knew he was being heard – he really knew he was being heard. When he concluded, Annoulis asked him if he would care for some refreshment.

He rang the bell and his maidservant appeared with coffee and sparkling water.

'My dear friend,' began Annoulis, 'I can see that you have suffered, and suffered very much. You are absolutely right in your pain because, without any doubt whatsoever, Cloggs's rights have been denied and he did not receive a fair hearing – not even close to it.'

The psychoanalyst was ashamed of himself at this moment because upon hearing these words, especially as they were said with such graceful authority and care, he openly wept.

'It's okay,' said Annoulis. 'Take your time.'

The psychoanalyst managed to compose himself and apologised.

'That's okay, it's understandable. In fact' – and here Annoulis chuckled – 'I am reminded a bit of myself, as a much younger man of course, when I see and hear you.' He was perhaps ten years older than the psychoanalyst, somewhere in his mid-seventies.

'Now,' said Annoulis with raised but appropriately grave sonority, 'let me tell you what I think.'

The analyst's heart was pounding with expectation as Annoulis shared his views.

'There are ethics in which you and I are considered experts, and there are politics. Here I would say that no one could claim expertise. From an ethical point of view, Slinder's actions and the Committee's behaviour were clearly wrong, but from a political point of view there is no doubt that it was the right thing to do. The world is always balanced between the ethical and the political, amongst other things: there are, of course, other balancings. But in the case of your

Society – which, as we know, has only some two hundred members – the issue is: if the Committee had found Bloggs's actions unethical, which they were, it would have very probably resulted in his being admonished or even thrown out of the UPS, and this would have had a devastating political effect on the Society. The Ethics Committee has *an ethical responsibility to the body politic* – not just to Cloggs and his particular issue. It had to take into consideration the effect such a finding would have on the ability of the Society to function. For example, I understand that Bloggs has eight candidates in personal analysis with him, so of course the Committee has had to think about the wider effects of an ethical action against Bloggs and how that would interfere with the analyses of these eight people. So it was not, at this point, a matter of "Cloggs vs Bloggs", but of "Cloggs vs Bloggs plus eight innocent human beings who would suffer horribly if Bloggs were found to be in the wrong".' Annoulis moved in his chair, so he looked more directly into the psychoanalyst's eyes, and continued. 'In addition, we are psychoanalysts, and as psychoanalysts we cannot ignore the psychic dimensions that affect our considerations. It is clear that Cloggs was unduly distressed by Bloggs's actions. He had an option to understand that Bloggs was just being Bloggs, and he could have left it at that, but he did not. In so doing, Cloggs *acted out* a part of himself that he simply could not control and he pushed this element *into the container* because he could not contain it himself. This, of course, as I understand from Slinder—'

'Wait a minute,' said the analyst, breaking in abruptly. 'You and Slinder have spoken about this?'

'Oh yes, of course.'

'But I thought this was confidential, our meeting.'

'Of course it is,' said Annoulis. 'Of course it is and will be. But I wanted to be absolutely sure about all the details of this issue, so I have done research which I consider appropriate to your situation and its gravity. Slinder, I assure you, is very aware of your concerns and she shares them herself.'

The psychoanalyst could feel the lower part of his body slide away.

'The point is,' Annoulis went on, 'that it is a matter of specifically psychoanalytical ethics to consider Cloggs's frame of mind and what he did to the Committee by bringing this matter before them, when he could have processed it himself. From a psychoanalytical perspective, was this an ethical action on his part – or did he fail as an ethical psychoanalyst? I think, given what we know of the unconscious, that this man had a grievance, that he invested in that grievance, that Bloggs simply became an internal object which Cloggs could not handle any longer and that, clearly, he had a sort of paranoid breakdown. This is why, is it not, as psychoanalysts we know that the overwhelming number of referrals we have to our Ethics Committees are driven by some paranoid state of mind in a figure like Cloggs.'

At this point Annoulis paused for several seconds, before continuing.

'You see, what we learn from psychoanalysis is that although from a superficial point of view Cloggs's complaint – that Bloggs had defamed him – was of course correct and just, when we look beneath the surface we see how such complaints are almost inevitably part of a pathological process; and thus Ethics Committees have a special responsibility to psychoanalysis at large to protect it from this sort of paranoid outburst. This is an additional dimension of what I mean by "the politics of ethics" in our profession. And, as I am sure you have considered, we cannot as psychoanalysts stop there: rather, we must ask even more penetrating questions. What is there about Cloggs's personality that led Bloggs to defame him? It is much too simple to say that Bloggs lost control of himself and carried out a campaign intended to slander Cloggs's reputation? Anyone can see that this is partly the case – but what we find, looking beneath the surface, is that Cloggs invited this attack on himself. Now, the lay person might ask how we know this and what evidence we have to substantiate such an observation. We do in fact have evidence, don't we, in Cloggs's attitude towards the Ethics Committee, because we can see from the reaction of the Committee, both to the original complaint and to Cloggs's subsequent communications, that he is an irritating man, a man who gets up people's noses, and who is clearly looking for trouble. Indeed, poor Bloggs – who is, I think, a brilliant and eminent thinker and a most influential person in our profession – fell prey to Cloggs's small-mindedness and has clearly been trapped – and I think Slinder's observations here are most interesting – by Cloggs's availability as a victim. So you see, my dear friend, there is nothing for you to worry about. I assure you that you have done the right thing by bringing this entire sorry matter to my attention, and I think it gives us not only cause for reflection but an opportunity to consider how we may improve matters for the future of psychoanalysis.'

Annoulis rose very graciously, extended his hand and guided the psychoanalyst to the front door, which opened onto the sunshine of a still brilliant Greek afternoon. As Annoulis bid his visitor goodbye, he placed his hand very gently on the psychoanalyst's shoulder and said that he was pleased to be able to tell him that the President of the UPS was going to invite the psychoanalyst to serve on the International Ethics Committee, but, and he winked, of course the psychoanalyst did not know about this yet. Annoulis chuckled and waved to the analyst, who was walking quickly towards the end of the house's gravel pathway.

The psychoanalyst was in a daze, and he was nearly hit by several cars as he crossed the street and began to hurry towards his hotel. Something was terribly wrong – he could feel it. For the first time since his adolescence he threw up suddenly and violently on the pavement, outside a greengrocer's and next to a tobacco kiosk. Partly covered in his own vomit, which was now dripping down his arms and his trouser leg, the analyst apologised in English and ran towards his hotel, which he reached before vomiting again. He managed to walk into the shower, fully clothed, and then collapsed.

When he came to, the water was running cold. He felt incredibly weak; he leant over to turn off the tap and slowly peeled away his wet suit. Once towelled dry, he climbed into bed and fell asleep, not waking until ten the next morning, having slept for fifteen hours.

The psychoanalyst knew that the Catastrophe had changed the course of the world's moral direction. In effect all of us were now without a moral compass. But he had always lived within the assumption – clearly naïve – that he was part of a moral or an ethical profession. He had always held psychoanalysis in such high esteem, certainly as a young man. But over the years the wars between the various movements, and the growing shoddiness of the so-called 'profession' of psychoanalysis had sickened him increasingly. And now, he reflected, the horror of his complicity in the violation of Cloggs's rights and the logic of Paris Annoulis, who clearly had already talked to everyone on his own Society's Ethics Committee, felt unbearable. What was he to do now – now that he could no longer believe in the ethical process of his own profession?

Or did it not matter?

And why was he so taken by this issue now?

The phone rang. It was Murk, obviously still very distressed by their previous encounter. The psychoanalyst, balancing the delicate scales of confidentiality, said that he should not worry about it. He should not worry, because the issue was taken care of and Murk should forget the whole thing.

Their conversation was interrupted by the most powerful noise the psychoanalyst had ever heard. It was like the noise of a passenger train roaring headlong into a station, crashing through concrete barriers, thudding through the station halls and offices, and roaring on into the streets. It was not a single sound, but a sound that contained in its belly a hundred different after-sounds and surround-sounds, and it was so unfamiliar that the psychoanalyst felt immediately sick.

It was Murk who spoke first.

'Oh my God.'

'I agree.'

'It could only have been . . .'

'A bomb.'

'A very large bomb.'

Within a few seconds they both heard the sound of sirens wailing their way from different parts of the city up to their area. The psychoanalyst no longer felt himself as existent; he had become a disembodied being, hanging by some thin, invisible thread.

'This was your patient,' said Murk.

'You know nothing,' said the psychoanalyst.

'It had to be your patient.'

'Murk, you know nothing.'

'Well if I know nothing, then how do I know that that was a bomb and that furthermore I know who did it?'

'I'm not listening to this any more.' With this the analyst hung up the receiver, his hand trembling. He ran out of his office, west toward Lahr Road, and expected to see the police station completely blown up. Instead it was intact – but next to it, where there had been a medium-sized park, there was now only a crater. To his shock, but also to his enormous relief, he could see Kalid al Walid in handcuffs being led off to a waiting police van. The press were of course already there, the police ordering them to move away from the area. Everyone seemed to be running about – people screaming, children crying, parents terrified that their children might have been in the park – and a police announcement was playing again and again over a loudspeaker: 'Ladies and gentlemen, please leave the area and go home. We have intercepted a potential act of terror with the controlled explosion of a device that was set to go off. We cleared the park and no one has been injured. Please leave the area and go home.'

126

All that the psychoanalyst could remember was the phrase 'set to go off'. It caused his legs to buckle. What did that mean? They were not meant to go off in a pre-set manner, he thought. Weren't they meant to be detonated by the bomber? There must be a new kind of vest that works according to a timer. Maybe Walid was so confident he would go through with his task that he pre-set it – or, on the contrary, maybe his cohorts were so doubtful about him that they pre-set it. Perhaps he never even knew it was pre-set?

A disturbing number of hours passed by before the psychoanalyst finally heard on the late evening news a report of what had happened. A man had entered the police station and calmly told everyone that he was wearing a martyr's vest. The desk sergeant, assuming it was a joke, had roared with laughter. Apparently this greatly disturbed the bomber – although they wondered now what kind of a bomber he was – because he yelled 'no golden teeth!' before tearing off his coat and ripping off his shirt to reveal the vest. A member of the Bomb Squad quickly detected that it had a timer set to go off in fifteen minutes, so they ran to the adjoining park, cleared it of people, threw the vest down the twenty-foot 'wishing well' and ran for cover.

As the days passed Walid's identity was revealed. The news reports said that he did not seem to be a real terrorist at all, but someone quite deranged: he talked incessantly about people laughing at him and about the laughter turning into balls of human flesh that rolled down a hill and turned into pomegranate trees that bled every twenty-eight days. The people living in the area of the park were relieved to discover that this was, after all, just an act of human madness and not predetermined evil.

The psychoanalyst, of course, was now in a different dilemma. He knew that Walid was indeed a terrorist and no doubt part of a cell, but because Walid was (he hoped at least) a former patient of his, he did not know how to inform the authorities that there really was a risk. In fact, as he had wiped Walid's memory clean of his terrorist background he could, he thought, be found to have assisted in the removal of vital evidence. He was also acutely distressed by the fact that he was profoundly ambivalent about suicide bombers. On the one hand he obviously found them terrifying, but he also felt that these poor sods – *sans* helicopter gunships, fighter aircraft, missiles, ordinary ordinance and armies – had nothing else to fight with except their own bodies. In some horrifying respect he knew that his 'work' with Walid was a multiple act of betrayal. He had denied this man's political position, which he degraded into a joke against what Walid now saw as his military duty. He had also ridiculed Walid's faith, and the analyst could take only small comfort in the fact that, at least at this stage in his life, he found *all* of the world's monotheistic religions profoundly sick.

Then there was Murk. Not only was he of no help, he was hysterical with anxiety. In the analyst's living room on the night of the bomb, Murk had tackled him again. The analyst reiterated that Murk knew nothing, but Murk insisted he did know and should say something to the authorities. Against his better judgement, the analyst then did something he would come to regret: he made an interpretation – indeed, a rather vicious one.

'So you know what they'll think when you say that, don't you?'

'When I say what?' Murk asked.

'When you say that you *know* the details?'

'They'll ask me to tell them.'

'That's right. And what will you be able to tell them?'

'That I know the analyst who was treating this guy.'

'No, you know the analyst who you *thought* was treating this guy.'

'But they will come to you.'

'I will say that I cannot discuss any patients with them,' the analyst said, 'and I will show them the ACIP policy document. I will then say that they should obviously question you further, because clearly you know something and you are therefore the one who should be investigated.'

'What?'

'Well, when someone says that they *know* all about it, the police can draw only one real conclusion.'

'What?' said Murk again.

'Either you are a publicity-seeking screwball – which, incidentally, is not far off – or you are party to information which you refuse to disclose, and you will then become a suspect.'

'This is just gibberish.'

'No, Murk. Think about it. Did I ever say to you that I was seeing a terrorist?'

'No, but you had that look in your eye.'

'I had the look of your projection,' said the analyst.

'The look of what?'

'Two things.'

'What two things?' Murk asked, clearly confused.

'Well, first, you were terrified and you projected that into me. But the only reason you had a look of terror is that you projected into my supposed patient the violent bomb-carrying part of your own personality. You saw what you wanted, or didn't want to see, by putting it into me. In other words, Murk, you are a fucked-up mess, which shouldn't take you too much by surprise, now, should it?'

Murk was too dumbfounded to speak at first. Instead he just stared at the analyst in a somewhat worrying way, and for a nanosecond the analyst feared he might unwittingly have hypnotised a second person. Then Murk said: 'You know, you really are a sick fuck. You shouldn't be practising.'

What the analyst did to Murk was, of course, a crime of sorts. It was in fact a crime which, ironically, he felt too many of his colleagues were committing on a regular basis: treating the patient's sense of reality as if it were simply projective. Indeed, if one good thing did come out of this sorry and fearful episode, the psychoanalyst thought, it was that he had become more fully conscious that he had been depressed for some time by life in his profession – and, more to the point, by life in institutions in general. Just being a member of a nation was depressing in itself, he thought. Thank God he was not part of Superpower; but his country was on Superpower's right shoulder, all perky and perched for purchasing the future of Superpower's wealth. One way or another we were all part of institutions – hospitals, corporations, institutes – and we all made the same unconscious mistake, he mused. We thought these places were somehow 'human'; we celebrated the birthdays of such places, we felt proud allegiance to them, and we filled their hallways with portraits of past leaders. In fact, a healthy institution – one not seriously ill by virtue of the pathology of group life – was a rarity on this earth.

But the analyst had decided that his free associations on the day of the bomb, especially to his meeting with Annoulis, must have been significant. To have been thinking of the illness of his own psychoanalytical Society, and further, to have realised that he was depressed because he was part of a fascist structure – this was an important recognition. In the days that followed he talked to colleagues about these ideas. Most of them said that one could not change society, that it made no sense, and the analyst could detect the same kind of fear he felt in himself: the fear that one would somehow be destroyed if one tried to escape the camp of persecution.

5

Bring back the muse

It was hard for the psychoanalyst to pay close attention to what William Glastonbury was saying in the following week's group discussion. His colleagues had decided to devote themselves to depression, as the previous meeting had seemed so productive. Even Sally Forensic became an enthusiastic supporter of this focus and recommended that the group should remain in depression for some months to come. Carson Walleye was beside himself with clinical examples celebrating the psychodynamics of depression.

But the analyst's thoughts were frequently elsewhere; he forgave himself his lapses, as the events of the previous week were still numbing. His 'treatment' of Walid was surreal yet, as a form of madness within the real, he hoped it would set itself off – as all traumata do – as a form of the unbelievable. Yet he knew that later, in the *après-coup*, a second event would set off Walid in front of him and he would pay for his comparative absence of emotion. He and Murk had avoided one another but he knew that they would meet up in the near future. Murk, for all his annoyances, was not someone glued to past injuries. He would simply transform the event into a script and it would show up on stage or on TV.

Ironically enough the psychoanalyst found himself

mulling over the depression of the unspeakable. Lacan had made a big deal about the rift between the imaginary (the image or the world of our imaginings), the symbolic (language representing it), and the real (the thing-ness presumed to be imagined or uttered) but the psychoanalyst found himself thinking of the 'unthought known' – that which we know, but which we have not thought. As Glastonbury droned on about depression, the psychoanalyst wondered about the strange reality of the unconscious, that part of us that perceives, organises and largely creates our world, but which does so without much of our consciousness in on the act. 'It's so weird,' he thought.

'What's weird?' asked Sally, startling the analyst, who realised he had spoken out loud.

'Um . . . it's weird that we cannot speak what we know because what we know is not available to consciousness. This is surely rather depressing – something of a universal depression, it seems to me.'

'I think what you say must be linked to what we've been talking about,' said William Glastonbury rather slowly, and with something of a distanced tone of voice. 'We've been discussing why we think the word "affect" is so crude and not up to describing what your patient "X", for example, has been going through. Indeed, your list of Ds is a kind of logic of emotion and Sally, I think, believes that the word "emotion" – from *movere* – is much closer to the human truth of depression because it conveys the fact that it is a moving experience.'

'Yes, and it's one that people would seem to want to stop, to arrest, through Napalmtrek® or any of the other anti-depressants,' added the psychoanalyst.

'But surely,' interjected Carson Walleye, 'anti-depressants are highly useful.'

'No doubt,' said the analyst, 'but only up to a point. After a while they decrease in effectiveness, as we know. But more importantly I think that as a *cultural phenomenon*, if I may put it that way, anti-depressants target emotional life itself, especially in countries like America, where it is considered unseemly to have an emotional life.'

'Is that what you meant by weird?' asked Sally Forensic.

'No, well, I found myself thinking of Eliot's words in "Prufrock": "I have heard the mermaids singing, each to each" – and his rather mournful next line, "I do not think that they will sing to me." But my thought was to substitute this with "I do not think that I will sing to them" because none of us can, you see.' The group looked puzzled and there was a silence. The psychoanalyst continued. 'I cannot speak my unconscious knowledge and, as I know this, I am excluded from the imaginary possibility of such a song. I believe that as we all suffer from this gap between what we know but cannot think, much less speak, and the little we do know and speak, we are all liable to depressions arising from this divide. Whitman cries out "I sing the body electric" and *Leaves of Grass* is a kind of miracle of conveyance: it is remarkable how much he churns out of himself; and our creativities, whatever they be, are noble efforts.'

'Yes, think of Shakespeare or Dostoevsky,' said Glastonbury.

'But they all knew that what they wrote was paltry in the face of the unthought known,' insisted the analyst.

'Isn't your commentary simply a variant on the old existentialist lament that we are born only to discover that we are doomed to die, and that our life is absurd as a result of this mixed blessing?' asked Glastonbury.

'Well, I think the existentialist lament is an important thinking of ontological depression, but I'm talking about something different. Why, for example, did I feel my life change in 1966 when I heard Leonid Kogan perform the Beethoven violin concerto?'

'What comes to mind?' asked Sally Forensic.

'Well, not much. That's the problem. I'd not heard of him before the concert, so there was the factor of the unknown: I was profoundly surprised by his interpretation and the ethereal tone he evoked from his violin. But still, why should I feel that this one moment was seminal?'

'Surely it is analysable,' said Carson.

'I'm sure we can make it into a meaning, but in my view that is simply cheating. I believe that whatever happened then was simply an ordinary, everyday event writ large – a happening that changed me, that could not escape consciousness, even if consciousness did not know what it meant.'

'And why is this depressing? What does this say about depression?' asked Glastonbury, now a little bit irritated by what he took to be a divergent train of thought.

'I think this relates to depression – to our topic – in that we are alone even from within,' said the analyst. 'Imagine the unthought known is an internal canon – knowledge of the self, all we have seen and created in ordinary apperception – and let us assume for a moment that we call this "the self" and when "we" (a split-off part of the self having a thought about itself) view our self, we can see nothing, even though we know, we know, that we are inhabited by . . .'

135

'What, by the proverbial "ghost in the machine"?' chuckled Glastonbury.

'Well, maybe so,' said the psychoanalyst. 'Maybe that is exactly what I mean. Perhaps the ghost is not the lost soul, a transient figure in a journey between the real and the afterlife. Perhaps the ghost is our very own self.'

'Jungians might say our "shadow",' added Sally.

'Well maybe, and if so, hooray!' said the analyst, a bit distracted because he was always aware of being Jung-deficient – in fact, this haunted him for much of his life. 'But we live with an ever-present sense of loss, because of course we wish we could know our self, not as an academic ambition, but as a form of intrapsychic marriage. After all, at the end of our days we are our own best companion, but—'

'But wait a minute!' interjected Sally. 'What makes you think we know those with whom we live? Perhaps you pine over loss of access not simply to your own good self but to your wife, your children . . . even us!' The group roared with laughter and then became collectively embarrassed, following which there was a long and discomforting silence.

'Well, I think this rather proves the point,' said the psychoanalyst. 'That we are alone, that we cannot really contact our others, including our self as our other. Yet I am unaware of any society that consciously recognises this, or that uses its politics to work towards offsetting the despair intrinsic to such loss.'

'But surely the world religions are there to effect exactly that,' said Glastonbury. 'Setting aside the view that religion is the opiate of the masses, our invention of a divine being, of God, is precisely designed to offer our self that other-who-knows-everything. Although we cannot know actual others

136

like this, although we cannot even know our self like this, we can nonetheless imagine a companion for our self.'

'God as imaginary companion?' asked Sally.

'Yes, if you will: God as imaginary companion. We pray not merely in order to establish a line of faith, although I expect that is one of the reasons, but we pray because we believe He knows all there is to know about the self. He is in on every detail of our experience.'

'Well,' said the psychoanalyst, 'I have always thought this was more than a bit unreal, even more outlandish than the idea that Santa Claus could somehow climb down all the chimneys of the Christian world on Christmas Eve and deposit his gifts. It's an absurdity to believe in an "all-knowing God", but it's a sensible wish, and the world's religions are beaming out the message – hoping that somewhere in the cosmos there is indeed a kind of divine intelligence that is capable of knowing all there is to know. In fact, we are never known like this – and personally I don't think anyone actually believes in God, even though they say they do. Belief in God is a wish for the arrival of an other who would presume to know us.'

The psychoanalyst paused, but no one said anything, so he continued. 'Actually, what is troubling about the Judaic, Christian and Muslim religions is that they divest selves of responsibility for the self's psyche, handing it over to a powerful Father.'

'I'm not sure,' said Glastonbury. 'In fact it seems like the reverse – that God, or Allah, presumes we are incapable of responsibility but demands it of us if we are to gain admission to Heaven or Paradise.'

'Yes, but the problem is that ironically, in submitting ourselves to these systems, and to monotheism, we actually divest ourselves of the internal father, that part of our mind that would hold us responsible for our actions.' The psychoanalyst went on to discuss Islam and in particular the Koran, arguing that each of the analysts in the room should read it in order to discover not only just how powerful Allah was, but also how deeply Muslims believed in Paradise. At least twenty-five percent of the book, he pointed out, was devoted to descriptions of Paradise or Hell. Muslims believed that during the course of their lifespan one angel sat on their right shoulder recording their good deeds, while another angel sat on their left shoulder recording their bad deeds, and on the Day of Judgement the book of their life would be presented to Allah, who would decide whether they were to go to Paradise or to Hell. He said that they should see just how precise the descriptions were of this Paradise – far more precise than the Christian concept of Heaven – and how interesting it was that, once in Paradise, Muslims could drink wine and have casual sex with slaves who were meant to serve their every need. You would never have any difficulty comprehending why people of the Islamic faith could become suicide bombers, the analyst said, given that such martyrdom entitled them to occupy the higher reaches of the seven levels of Paradise – rather like being on one of the more expensive floors of the best five-star hotel in the world.

In the weeks to come the psychoanalysts took his advice and, after reading the Koran, they discussed the 'religious solution', as they temporarily called it – a 'compromise formation' between the absence of value (or conscience) and an overwhelming moral existence. In effect, the monotheistic religions assumed that men and women were psychopaths, and indeed, these faiths – utterly dependent on a powerful God – could only be constructed by psychopaths who projected their conscience (now absent) into God. The only reason believers believed was because they were terrified that this all-knowing God would punish them by sending them to Hell one day: hardly an advertisement for the meritorious dimensions of conscience itself.

But what did this have to do with depression?

It was inevitable that such religions would predispose believers to depression, not simply because it assumed the worst of humankind, but because the proffered solution – the Day of Judgement – ironically incarcerated believers in a psychopathically constructed drama that tied them to a powerful father figure, from whom they could never escape. Both Christians and Muslims could demonstrate godliness through good deeds or prayer, leading them to think of themselves as good people and thus offsetting the harsher sides of depression. But in the end such footnotes to the system failed and left all believers with a hopeless dilemma: to believe was to submit to a theology that derived its energy from the assumption that men and women left to themselves (without God or Allah) would wander into evil, and therefore one had to remain forever dependent.

Later the psychoanalyst realised that such powerful gods had to exist precisely because no one could truly internalise these irrational religions. They obviously could not be trusted to accept the tenets of these systems of belief because such systems would not survive mental scrutiny. So the 'believers' had to live in fear of a powerful judgement, in that as they really could not believe, they could only be found out as non-believers and sent to Hell for it. Eventually the religions wore down the 'believers' and after while, as to thinking for oneself – well, who *could* believe in that?

It was after leaving one of these discussion groups a few weeks later that the psychoanalyst had a late afternoon coffee with Val Vacto, to discuss her book on mental slavery. She had convinced several eminent authors to contribute to the book and, upon hearing of the psychoanalyst's interest in depression, had asked him to coffee so that they could talk about the cultural aspects of depression. Sitting in Hippo, they began by reviewing *Down On Myself*, the remarkable autobiography by the African-American psycho-historian Samuel Fuller. The drive behind Fuller's book was a near-suicidal depression experienced in his early fifties. He could barely function and he sought psychoanalysis, after which he wrote not only about his own life but about the lives of African-Americans and other oppressed people.

Fuller began with why it was that he had married a woman who was – as one friend put it – a 'slave-driver', a remark that hit Fuller between the eyes. His wife was indeed an unusually imperious figure, who ran the household as if it were a plantation and her husband a field slave. Fuller had been raised in a matriarchy dominated by his grandmother, his three aunts and his mother. As long as he did what they said, he was fine. As a child he was an outstanding student and athlete, and after gaining his PhD in history he went straight into a marriage that replicated life in the matriarchy.

Fuller examined why his grandmother and the other women in his family were so demanding. He used Anna Freud's concept of 'identification with the aggressor' to argue that as African-American women they had to incorporate into their child-rearing techniques the terms of enslavement to which they had been indentured in the years of real slavery under the white landowners. On the plantation such women had to be very harsh on their children, in order to protect them from being killed by the white population, and the psychology of protection was to incorporate some of the terms of oppression as forms of inoculation, so that the children would not step out of line.

Thus even though actual slavery was long since gone, argued Fuller, it was sustained psychologically in many African-American families by this transgenerational communication.

How had Samuel Fuller sustained slavery?

Even though he was a brilliant historian, Fuller fell behind in his academic work. He was often late for class, he got behind in grading papers, he had dozens of half-completed essays in his desk but was not publishing anything and, of course, although his colleagues indicated concern from time to time, Fuller needed no external reproach because he was paralysed by a sense of failure. That is, until he realised that he had in fact over-committed himself, setting up a structure that would inevitably leave him thinking he was incompetent. Furthermore, on his return home from the university every day, his wife would berate him for his inadequacies at work, and she would successfully argue that were it not for her he would be an absolute basket case. As the years passed Fuller became convinced that his existence depended on his wife's ministrations; she would sit him down at the kitchen table and force him to grade papers, refusing to go on summer holidays unless his work was completed, and she insisted he finish at least one essay every two years.

Fuller argued that although he had unconsciously selected a wife who was personally predisposed to sustaining the matriarchy, his 'passive aggression' against her oppression brought out the worst in her and made her even more dominating. Indeed, he came to see that it suited him to stay on the 'plantation' and force his wife into the role of 'slave-driver', until depression struck.

'It's interesting,' said Val Vacto, 'that were it not for his depression, Fuller might never have objectified his oppression.'

'I agree,' said the analyst. 'He *should* have been depressed by what he had set up for himself and, because depression is *always* a cocktail of many other affects and ideas, his depression was like a puzzle that needed unpacking.'

'And you would agree,' she said, 'that when he thought of killing himself – which he made sure his wife knew about time and again – he was being sincere, and yet he was enacting something at the same time.'

The analyst nodded.

'But if that is so,' she continued, 'how do you distinguish between this individual suicidal thinking and suicide as a cultural statement?'

'Well, it's a good question. I think Fuller had really had it with his life. He saw no way out because he could not resolve the depressions. Indeed, part of his argument in the book is that even when he did well – and we know some of his essays won prizes – he could not accept the praise of his colleagues, on the grounds that he was an impostor.'

'Yes, he wrote that this was a genuine feeling,' said Val, 'but came to understand this conviction as a demand on his part that he not be taken for granted as a success, that as a slave he was actually still on the plantation, and any notion that he was somehow capable of doing well was based on errors of perception.'

'So he thought of suicide because he really could not see a way forward,' continued the analyst. 'But in thinking of killing himself and letting his wife know about this, he became aware that he was using the threat of suicide as a homicidal act against his wife . . .'

'Which set him free.'

'Yes,' said the analyst, 'which set him free . . . once he *understood* this was what he was doing. Because until he grasped it – and he hints that this occurred in his analysis – he had to disguise the wish for freedom inside the notion of mental illness, of a depression driving him to death, a state of mind and a voice that his wife willingly accepted, as it perpetuated the legacy of his being incompetent.'

'Indeed,' said Val. 'To the point where he was unable to keep himself alive. So . . . when he left his wife – not impulsively, but thoughtfully – he not only reversed his depression but he broke out of cultural oppression at the same time.'

'Yes, I think that's the point where he decided to write his autobiography, because he reckoned this was a situation that other African-American men, as well as men and women of other races who had been victims of oppression, were carrying inside them, and it was best to write it so that others could gain a deeper understanding of the "depths of depression".'

'Ah, yes,' said Val. 'It's interesting, isn't it, that contained in that wisdom is an intrinsic understanding that depression is indeed *deep*.'

'A lot deeper than Napalmtrek® can reach,' replied the analyst.

Val Vacto asked him what other cultural theorists should be included in her book. She thought Fuller might write a short essay, or at least agree to be interviewed, but what about Martha Weinrob? Weinrob's book, *Recreating Auschwitz*, was still so shocking that Val was afraid it might be too hot to handle. She wanted to know in what way Weinrob's ideas related to depression because, although she had used many psychoanalytical arguments in her analysis of Israeli 'foreign policy', Weinrob had not addressed the question of depression explicitly. Val thought there was a similarity between Fuller's concept of self-enslavement, derived from transgenerational perpetuation of the terms of oppression, and Weinrob's analysis of Israel.

'Well, first let's review Weinrob's position,' said the analyst, with a wave over Val's shoulder to Gideon, who was walking up the street. 'Her argument is that a "collective epiphany" occurred in Israel upon the construction of the Wall surrounding the country.'

'Upon construction of the Wall with the towers,' added Vacto.

'Yes, that's right. It was the publication of that famous photo of the Wall and a tower that iconically captured the fact that the Israelis had reconstructed Auschwitz and put themselves back inside the concentration camp. At least, that's Weinrob's analysis . . .'

'Which she argues is valid because even some Israeli writers reacted this way upon seeing the photo.'

'Yes,' said the analyst, 'but part of her argument would be that even though people *knew* this was true, analytically speaking the building of the Wall was so deeply unconscious an action that they refused to know what they knew.'

'I wanted to talk to you about that,' said Val. 'She argues that the Likud government played upon a collective negative hallucination: the denial that the Palestinians existed. The continual use of this form of defence became so pervasive that the Israeli leaders were able to blind the population to a strategy that would in the end not simply fail, but that would recreate a world of hate that itself put the Jewish people back into a concentration camp. This was accomplished via a kind of collective sleepwalking led by the government. Is that what she's saying?'

'That's about it,' replied the analyst. 'Weinrob believes that the fundamentalist religious zealots in Israel constantly played upon the Zionist notion that they were the "chosen people", in effect eradicating any opposition. Importantly, however, she does acknowledge that Israelis had reason to fear the extremist Palestinians and others in the region who, from the beginning, wanted to annihilate Israel . . .'

'And that cannot be an easy position to be in,' added Val.

'Absolutely. But it didn't take a genius to see that the only real solution for Israel was to make peace with the Palestinians, and Weinrob's point is that intellectual genocide – the mental eradication of the Palestinians – led to a shift in Israeli mentality: the negative hallucination meant that they also got rid of those parts of the political mind that might have been able to see that such a strategy would fail. Of course, as we know, killing off an entire people in one's mind erodes the self, and so this has led to a kind of collective depression in Israel. These are a highly moral and honourable people and for them to find themselves committing genocide was a terrible psychic catastrophe. The motivation for the Wall may have been to protect them, but in fact what it did was to cut them off from the outside world and leave them incarcerated.'

'I was talking to Rosalind Royce,' said Val, 'and she believes that Weinrob has left out an important piece of the puzzle. I thought I could ask her to contribute a chapter.'

'What does she say?'

'Well, Rosalind Royce says that the concept of negative hallucination leaves out something even more troubling.'

'More troubling than intellectual genocide?' asked the psychoanalyst.

'Yes. She was not talking specifically about Israel, but about Superpower, and about one country's total domination of another. Her argument is that it is pleasurable. Her essay would state that the unconscious reason why people go to war with one another – like Superpower's beating up of other countries, or Israel's military domination of the Palestinians – is that hate is pleasure. She uses the analogy of football matches, saying that fans love to hate the opposition, especially if it is a long-standing rivalry; that people go to football matches in part because of the pleasure of pure hate.'

The psychoanalyst was impressed by this line of thought, and before he left he urged Val to see if Rosalind Royce would write an article on hate. It made a lot of sense and reminded him of his own view that Superpower and its enemies were destroying otherness by turning one another into hated mental objects. He was sure that if people could just get to know one another, hang out with each other, it would reverse the process of 'objecthood' – the murder of otherness through transformation into a mere object. But he had failed to appreciate the engine of such destruction, that hate was a pleasure. One could dump all of one's shit into the other, he thought, project whatever one wanted into the enemy, who was then simply to be eradicated or disposed of. That was of course what happened in the Holocaust: the Nazis delighted in hating the Jews and could not give this pleasure up.

The psychoanalyst's grandfather and uncles on his father's side of the family were Jews and his grandfather, who was an anti-Zionist, had been an enormous influence in his childhood. He was struck not simply by his grandfather's gentleness and wisdom, but by his insistence that we must never fail to confront hate wherever it resides. The analyst was sure that his grandfather would have been horrified, were he alive, to see Israel waging such hate against its neighbours.

The psychoanalyst and Westin had agreed to meet up after work that evening for a drink, and even though he knew Westin was profoundly pro-Israel, and even an articulate apologist for Superpower, he reckoned he would try some of this thinking on his friend. He wasn't surprised, however, that Westin found the argument typical of the dangers of psychoanalytical thinking: on what evidence could the analyst base such claims? Westin knew that this question always rather flummoxed the analyst, who was never very good at defending what he took to be insight.

'But are you seriously suggesting,' asked Westin, 'that Superpower takes pleasure in hating enemies?'

'Yes, I am.'

'But that's absurd – Superpower has no vested interest in hating anyone. To the contrary, Superpower has all the reason to befriend the world – making it safe so that its markets can prosper. It has no interest in alienating other countries, much less taking pleasure in it!'

'Well,' the analyst replied, 'you're right that it doesn't make sense – but countries are not always "logical" and in this case I think the pleasure of hating others exceeds the national interest in befriending the world.'

'So you think that if Superpower just nuzzled up to a dictator here or a dictator there and said "why not be friends?" its enemies would turn to jelly, get all gooey with affection and just lose the totalitarian parts of their minds?'

'Well, to some extent that's what happened between Reagan and Brezhnev,' said the analyst. 'They got on with each other. It wasn't Superpower's military domination of the Soviets that won the Cold War, it was the development of friendship. Then those within the Soviet Union who favoured better relations were able to capitalise on the power of goodness, just as Nixon had done with China.'

'Oh, come off it,' said Westin. 'You can't tell me that if Superpower courts the extremists who want to destroy it, they are suddenly going to cave in to the hitherto unsuspected love they hold towards Superpower, and just drop their plans to wreak revenge?'

Before the analyst could reply, Westin cut him off by trying to change the topic: 'Anyway, I thought you were into depression – what the hell has this got to do with depression, and why do you always end up going off on a tangent?'

'Ah, well,' the analyst said, 'if we, as citizens of these countries, collude with a political process that is hate-based rather than love-based then we know, unconsciously, what we're up to. We know that we're taking pleasure in turning people into enemies; indeed, that we even take pleasure in our enemy's hatred of us, because then we gain further licence to murder more of them. And, even though we would of course deny this and defend our actions as necessary or even noble, we cannot fool the part of our personality that judges us – and that part of us knows what we're up to and finds what is in our hearts to be despicable. So we then fall out of ordinary love with ourselves and we become empty vessels – hollow men. Having emptied ourselves of our love, we are loveless souls. Indeed, Rathbone Krisk, in his book *We Are the Walking Dead*, argued that the "walking dead" film genre which burgeoned towards the end of the Vietnam War objectified the loss of the American soul. The dead parts of the self were now the dominant population and those who were living were trapped. Looked at another way, the walking dead were the unrecognised, depressed parts of the living. Incidentally, this was also the time when America fell in love with anti-depressants.'

The psychoanalyst was rather hurrying his arguments at this point, because he could see that Westin was becoming impatient and was on the verge of cutting their beer time together. He could also tell that Ali, the barman in the Old Bush, was put off by the overly serious nature of their conversation, which he always reckoned put others off their drink. So the analyst stopped, shrugged his shoulders, and told Ali that in truth he found even talking about it depressing.

'Of course it's depressing,' replied Ali.

'Yes, I know,' said the analyst. 'But why do you think that is?'

'Well, the whole fucking world is one depressing reality, isn't it?' said Ali, looking at Westin.

Westin pushed back from the bar, held out his hands and said: 'Look, I can see where this conversation is going and I'm off. Sure, we can all hang our heads in some form of self-pity, but I'm not into this, so see you in a day or two.' With that he walked out of the Old Bush.

'Shit mate, sorry. Didn't mean to put him off his drink!'

'Oh, it's not your fault,' replied the analyst. He stuck around for another fifteen minutes or so before he left for a leisurely walk home. He had to admit to himself that Westin Moorgate had a point. Was the analyst coveting self-pity? Anyway, he asked himself, what was self-pity? Of course, in a superficial way he knew that it was sorrow directed toward the self, a kind of mothering of the self – 'oh you poor, poor dear' – but he wondered if there was some necessity to self-pity. When we took pity on others, it was not necessarily a bad thing, he thought, so why not take pity on the self? He then wondered if a distinction could be made between legitimate self-pity and false self-pity. Legitimate self-pity might well be an emotional experience and a form of relationship (between parts of the personality) necessitated by circumstances, while the false kind would be an exploitation of that otherwise necessary self-pity, one that earned it a bad name.

For it occurred to the analyst, as he paused outside the Telephone Store, that he did feel rather sorry for himself. He felt sorry that he had to live in these specific times, when the whole world really did seem to be falling to moral pieces. He was sorry that his profession seemed to be so shoddy and ill-deserving of respect – something he pined for but feared was never to be recovered. He was sorry that Westin Moorgate and others seemed so troubled by the agitations of conversation that they could bear only a few minutes' discourse on matters of grave importance. He was also sorry to be sixty-four; yes, absolutely sorry about that. Indeed, upon hearing this thought he felt very much in need of some cuddling other who would take him in her arms and tell him not to worry. It was that part, he realised, which must be the agent of self-pity, the part that took pity on us. Maybe, he wondered, to pity oneself was to be looked after by a muse who cared for one and who did so in silence. When we spoke up, as he had done at the Old Bush, we could be seen to reveal a type of intimate relation to ourself in the presence of the other – something that might have put Westin off.

Could it be that depression, a kind of self-pity saturated with sorrow, was a secular alternative to being looked after by a God? Given the rigours of ordinary human life, if we had to live them without a God, entirely within our own and our society's capabilities, maybe this gap was filled by a different kind of muse, a split-off part of the self that hung around in our time of need? Maybe our curiosity about this part could be such, thought the analyst, that we intensified our miseries just to see if this brought about self-pity and our muse? Was depression – the pressing under of the self by the weight of life – a kind of call for a higher entity that could bring us up again, could give rise to a new self? Certainly that must be one of the aims of the manic state of mind. And Napalmtrek® promised that for sure – but Napalmtrek® brought us up by exfoliating our mental life, he thought, so that all that remained was this kind of floating, superficial self that had lost its roots in the rest of the personality. But perhaps the muse who arrived to talk to us, indeed to feel sorrow for us, gave us a kind of hope that we could indeed be looked after.

Passing by Medici, looking at all the displays of various tiled rooms, the psychoanalyst was momentarily struck by the energy of the up-and-coming generations and all those blueprints for their future. As it was some time now since he had been actively engaged in bringing up his children, he had rather lost interest in such issues. But more recently he had begun to find that babies – in pushchairs, held by parents, sitting in cafés, plopped on carpets in their homes – were looking at him with a particular kind of intensity. For a while he took this to be simply a typical infant look, until he realised that 'they' saw him as different. In what way? In that he was old and grey, someone frail rather like they were, he wondered, a comrade in a world just beyond comprehension? A fellow traveller existing outside the bristling confidence of everyone aged between eleven and fifty-five? As time passed the analyst realised that rather than gaze at the parents, he always glanced at the infants – and he was sure they gave him the gestural equivalent of the high-five, a kind of 'hey dude, how's it going?' He found it wonderfully heartening.

So, he asked himself, is this it? I'm on the way out, they're on the way in, and we both know it?

They had mothers, of course, although in all kinds of form, but what did he have? No good saying he had a wife, or children, or friends: that was wonderful, he thought, but it did not touch the realm of his own isolation. Between his own being and his death, who was there? There was indeed a muse, he reckoned, as long as he did not call upon her in false circumstances. The death of a friend, the sudden eruption of a physical illness, the bizarre loss of memory in perfectly ordinary circumstances: these moments called the muse for him, like a kind of psychic 999 that brought an instant response. And when he heard from the muse – usually after much swearing on his part – he often heard the same voice and message: 'It's okay, don't worry; it's ordinary, part of the expected, so calm down and wait a bit.'

The previous week, for example, he had tripped on something while walking up the street – afterwards he realised it was only the pavement – and he careered headlong into a neighbour's peony, falling flat on his face. 'Are you all right?' voices asked, as three or four people came to his aid. They brought him to his feet but his shame never let him see their faces, although he thanked them. In fact, he found himself deeply shocked at his sudden loss of balance. Balance, he thought – fuck that. He could no longer even expect to walk the street without falling over, no matter how small the impediment.

But the muse came. Not to inspire creativity, but to console him for his losses. Was this self-pity? He doubted it. In a non-psychoanalytical group he might even have argued that it was a true other, not a split-off part of himself. But he knew he could not get away with that kind of view with analysts. There were no mysteries, no new-age funfairs, no muses; just projections here, or projections there, a kind of ballistic theory of meaning. When we thought we might be hearing from some other, some kind muse, some good soul looking after us, it was just another shot in the dark.

'I have heard the mermaids singing, each to each. I do not think that they will sing to me.' This refrain – hashed about by his need – banging around in his mind again. Why?

He had already established, he thought, that we humans were necessarily depressed because we were fated to a kind of aloneness for which there was no cure; but now he seemed to think otherwise. It was as if we were not truly alone, but the others who we yearned to speak to – and who we could overhear speaking to themselves – did not speak to us, and from us they could not hear. Was that why we worshipped dolphins and whales, he wondered, and even prairie dogs? They spoke to one another but not to us, even though they made noises we could hear. Was it not odd to spend so much time on this planet with all these other creatures, who surely enjoyed babbling to one another, but to be unable to get through to them? Images of chimps signing to their carers were wonderful and tempting objects of belief in some miraculous breakthrough to our fellow creatures – but he knew these were just amulets of hope. He knew there never would be a moment when a whale, a dolphin or a prairie dog would speak what he or she experienced as an existent.

'You seem quite troubled,' his daughter said, when she bumped into him a few yards from their home.

'God, you are right.'

'Well, come on, let's have a chat,' said Alice.

So they went into the house and she looked at him with eyes that were searching yet very still. He was struck by the fact of her beauty and the reality that every time he saw her she seemed even more beautiful than before. But this was one of those things in life, he thought, that could only be spoken in a casual, offhand sort of way. He could not, for sure, say to his daughter that she was one of the most beautiful women he had ever seen.

'Where are you?' she asked.

'Well, I don't know exactly, but I've been thinking about self-pity, and being without God – for me . . .'

'Tell me about it.'

'Yeah, well . . . I'm sorry.'

'For what?' asked Alice.

'Well, you know, not bringing you up to *believe*.'

'Well, if you had tried you would have failed. And in any case, you couldn't have done it.'

'I couldn't?'

'No. You were much too full of doubt, and anyway you would have been a bad example of a life of religious fortitude.'

'Not even for conversion?' he said. They both laughed. Then they were quiet for a bit and she asked again what was wrong.

To his utter shock, the psychoanalyst burst into tears. His daughter moved very gently to his side and held his head with her right arm. It was not intrusive; indeed, if a muse could have been there, this is how she would have functioned. Alice said nothing and he recovered, but he did not know what to say. She knew this, of course, as she knew him better than he recognised.

She said: 'Why not go up to dinner now and we can talk about this later.' It was a credit to her wisdom that she knew he could not speak and needed to 'move on', but this kind of understanding, he realised, was an increasingly rare intelligence in this world.

Dinner proved to be a lively affair. Two of his daughter's friends showed up at the last minute, but the analyst and his wife always seemed to be able to conjure meals out of thin air. He was happy as a lark after two glasses of his favourite red wine, and as he gazed about him at these beautiful, young, talented people – and looked across at his wife, his double in ontological status – he was someone reassured.

Afterwards he clambered up the steps to the bedroom and sat in a chair. His custom was to do this for half an hour or so before his wife joined him; he liked the peace of the afterwards and he also loved to hear the distant voices and laughter in the house. He knew he was seeking some kind of comfort found in the intimate absence of the other, some comfort in being part of the human race, of being a father, a husband, a friend. These half-hours were among the best moments of his life; he would carefully take off his clothes, sometimes just stare at his nude body, and on occasion, as tonight, talk to himself at length.

'It's a good evening, so why are you depressed?'

'I don't know. Further, it is fruitless to aim to know.'

'Why?'

'Because there are too many reasons.'

'So, you're depressed because there are too many dimensions to this?'

'No.'

'So, what then?'

'I have no idea.'

'That's not good enough. Your mind is functioning, so you have ideas. So when you think you are depressed, what comes to mind?'

'Well, it's rather obvious.'

'Oh yes?'

'I'm depressed – a word, mind you, that I reject, but fuck it: I'm depressed, because I am simply part of the life cycle.'

'Yes, but so what? You know that.'

'Yet knowing it and actually coming to the end of it are two very different things.'

'So toughen up, then.'

'I'm not sure I want to. I think the whole idea of being tough is nonsense.'

'Oh yeah, then what are you going to do: run home every time you have a sphincter crisis and feel you are on the verge?'

'Fuck that. I refuse that.'

'So what, then? What was that?'

'I have no idea, and anyway it doesn't matter.'

'What, the fact that you were out shopping and then thought all of a sudden that you were going to shit your pants, so you abandoned your plans and drove home – this was no big deal?'

'It's the life cycle. I have to get used to this. Only a few months ago I put my mother in diapers and learned to clean her body.'

'You're lying. You rationalise the biggest change in your life. You deny the depression of full recognition.'

'What is that?'

'It's the in-your-face knowledge that you are out of here.'

'Not yet.'

'Everything you do is now related, whether you like it or not, to your ending.'

'So what's new?'

'It's not new as an *idea*. As a *reality*, it's unprecedented.'

'I don't get it.'

'Remember all the times you would drop by the travel agent and pick up brochures on trips to Majorca, Tunisia, Morocco, the Seychelles, and so on, and so on?'

'Of course.'

'All the time, yes?'

'Often, certainly.'

'You were trying to defeat death by turning it into a tourist attraction. "The holiday of a lifetime", they all read: you can believe it.'

'You're full of shit.'

'I am you, authorised by you; so don't give me that.'

'So, what has this to do with anything?'

'Don't know. Remember . . .'

At this point a part of his mind played 'All I Have To Do Is Dream' and he was away for minutes that felt like hours.

The analyst awoke from his daydream and his conversations with himself and he went into the bathroom. He soaped up his face, brushed his teeth, and climbed into bed, where he was joined by his wife. Bed was the final solution. Dropping off to sleep, he wondered whether sleep itself was more of a solvent than the dream. To be left alone. Alone, even though in the presence of a loving other. Alone, yet protected by the belief that one would be here tomorrow.

Fortunately he awoke the next morning cured by sleep. Remarkable, he thought, how sleep cured one of ordinary woes. Thoughts of his depression were at least deferred until the next 'attack' and although he knew it would come, he also reckoned that he would be up for it. Later in the day, when thinking of the previous afternoon's breakdown, he would come up with a theory that these 'attacks' were preparations for the deepening crisis of age. Each crisis that brought on despair made him stronger and leaner, clearly preparing him for the end time.

He met Westin for their walk and this time they avoided anything heavy, concentrating instead on Westin's forthcoming book about the media. It was tentatively titled *You Call This 'Media'?* and Westin was a bit worried that this title might be giving away his entire thesis in a nutshell. That thesis was that we are lulled by the word 'media', which has a kind of onomatopoeic, soporific aspect to it that unconsciously convinces us that our perception of reality is really being mediated by a thoughtful process. Although Westin devoted chapters to the yellow journalism of the late nineteenth and early twentieth centuries, he argued that while today's print media betrayed bias and were clearly upfront, the television media – transmitted through these gorgeous men and women with sylvan voices – could be corrupt or psychotic and yet we would not know it. Indeed, the print media, he said, had taken a clue from this evolution and had now smartened up their fonts, come up with colourful pages, and tried to create the illusion of a soft presence.

In fact, Westin argued that the various forms of media were 'borderline', and he was in this respect quite grateful to the psychoanalyst for talking to him about the borderline personality. When Westin had heard the analyst's description of how borderlines are split personalities that take one view to the extreme and then flip to its opposite without any apparent bridge, Westin had cried out: 'Shit, that's the press!' And so his book gave example after example of how the television news would, for instance, decide that a political figure was a monster, vilifying him day after day until he quit office, whereupon they would suddenly focus on what a good person he was and how misunderstood his policies had been. As well as providing many samples of this borderline trait, Westin's book examined the notion that the people were expected to put their trust in the media. What did it mean, his book asked, to trust borderline perception as the mediator between self and the outside world? During his walk with the psychoanalyst he wondered whether, since he worked in the media, his book would have an adverse effect on his relations to colleagues.

'God, you can imagine the reviews,' he said.

'Oh, I don't know,' said the analyst, 'they may like it. After all, I'm not sure that the people who write for TV or the press will disagree at all. Imagine being told to tear into some poor jerk week after week and then after he is destroyed having to write sympathetic copy. You may find yourself becoming a hero.'

'I would find that pretty embarrassing. Anyway . . . I do the same thing. I flip from one side of an issue to the other, and any good reviewer will say that those who live in glass houses shouldn't throw stones.'

'Well, who cares?' replied the analyst. 'Today I'm off to see three people who are seriously depressed, and yesterday I got in quite a bad state myself.'

'You did?'

'Yup.' The analyst was not sure what to say and they walked in silence for a few minutes, passing by the duck pond that was way station to a flock of Canada geese. As was their wont, Westin Moorgate and the psychoanalyst leant against the railings and stared at the creatures.

'Well, I suppose it's reasonable for a person like yourself, a psychoanalyst, to get depressed, just like the rest of us. Why should you be any different?'

'Yes, I agree.'

'Shit, maybe it's the thought of having to see three depressed people,' said Westin. 'That alone would depress the hell out of me. I couldn't bear to be in the room with people throwing their problems at me. It's a lucky break that I can sit in my office and write about anything I like and I don't have to talk to anyone if I don't want to.'

That seemed to be the end of the conversation; they found themselves at the park gate and it was time to head off. The analyst's first patient was Myrna Fallbrook and he was in his office about fifteen minutes before she arrived. She had made considerable progress and today she was more upbeat than he had previously seen her. She now looked back on her depression with curiosity.

'I think I understand how I got to the point that I did. I hated it when you told me that I was "siding with my depression" but I knew you were right, I just didn't know why. I was saying to Acton, "Fuck you – okay, you're right, I am a screw-up, now watch this"; but this went underground and surfaced months later over a minor matter, when Acton was a long way away. I didn't know that my refusal to get out of bed, eat or go to work was a vegetative rebellion, another "fuck you", but this time a "fuck you" to the part of my mind that was exhorting me to get up and work. All that stuff you said about my being on strike made sense. But . . .'

'Yes?' asked the analyst.

'But there was something you were saying about how my depression was also a sign that I didn't want to think about my life. I've been pondering that but I can't quite get there. I know that my dad, who I love, never thinks about his life – or doesn't appear to want to – and when things went belly-up in our family, he was just stone cold and refused help of any kind. I know I'm a bit like that.'

'Well, if we don't allow ourselves to think about our painful experiences then in a way we consign ourselves to our moods, which are sort of storehouses of the forgotten.'

'And your point is that it won't work,' she said.

'Well, it works for a time, and for some people who get the diagnosis of depression this transformation can last a lifetime, with the self thinking that anti-depressants are the cure.'

'And you think that the anti-depressants are complicitous with the decision not to think.'

'Yes. I believe that when you suffered the original humiliation by Acton, you could not think about your feelings, much less talk to someone about them. That is because I think your family's tradition was not to talk about matters, and thus they avoided revealing patterns of thought through talking. As such, there was no apparent thought applied to lived experience, like when you won the tennis tournament but lost your best friend due to her jealousy. You couldn't talk this through with your mum and dad, and you couldn't think about it, so you just went on and ploughed through your future in a thoughtless way.'

'And so when I was an adolescent and got into terrible moods it was because I was not letting myself think about what was causing me to be so upset.'

'Exactly,' said the analyst. 'You were so angry with others, or yourself, that your revenge took the form of not thinking. Not to think was to put yourself in jail and throw away the key.'

'God, that's so true . . . I can recall knowing why I was upset and also feeling that the cause of the upset did not deserve any thought, that this would be a way of giving in to something.'

'Yes, it would have been giving in to the possibility of positive transformation, but of course when we're angry we aren't necessarily in a positive frame of mind. In your case, by the time you were an adolescent, you and your family were so furious with the work of the positive that you all stopped thinking and talking about what was distressing. Instead you turned yourselves into emotional robots and measured life's meaning through academic and sporting accomplishments.'

Myrna Fallbrook was a changed person: both she and the psychoanalyst knew this.

During an hour's break later that day, the psychoanalyst wrote in his notebook that unfortunately people were 'electing' depression over thought. The rise in depressions was simply an index of the fall in thinking. People were angry, yes, and not thinking was an expression of anger. But the issue was even wider and graver than that, he reckoned. There had been a cultural shift away from psychoanalysis, that in so many respects was a signifier for 'thinking about the self'. However much one might fault psychoanalysis for its failures – and, for sure, there were many – Freud-bashing and the worshipping of psychotropics were symptoms of a world turning away from contemplation. Psychoanalysis was the best medium for study of the self and now it was under attack. As a result, little thought was being applied to the problems of ordinary life, and thus affects were left as the dustbin of the thoughtless. At times the psychoanalyst was truly furious with this state of affairs; but he had studied history at university and he knew that there was really very little that one could do about it. Indeed, he would never know for certain – because he would not live long enough to see how things turned out – but he reckoned the world was rejecting thought with the same force that, long ago, it had rejected the Renaissance. Superpower's declaration that 'might made right' was simply an indicator of social solutions all over the world. Napalmtrek® and the other medications were very powerful, that was for sure, and people all around the world were now attacking their minds by drugging themselves into psychic oblivion.

These drugs might solve a certain type of depression for a certain period of time. The analyst had no problem conceding that. But the irony was that as depressions were in fact inoculative, they helped human beings cope with the ardours of life. So these anti-depressants were actually disabling people – dulling their receptive capabilities and preventing them from experiencing life moments.

He knew many would disagree with this. Indeed, some months earlier he had been visited by Enid Sullivan, a prominent writer who sought him out because she had heard from Fred Murk that the analyst believed anti-depressants were the bringers of thoughtlessness. He recalled their heated conversation.

'I'm here because Mr Murk told me of your views,' she had begun, 'and I am more than willing to pay your fee for the hour simply to tell you that I believe your views are incredibly irresponsible. I have been depressed for thirty years. I was in therapy for twenty-five years, and it was no help at all. The only reason I can function now is because I'm on Zenon – which has saved my life. You can't possibly understand what depression feels like. It is completely incapacitating. If you had ever felt this way, and I mean totally stopped in your tracks, then you would know what I'm talking about; but you have obviously never suffered from depression and don't have a clue what it feels like.'

'Do you remember the first time you were depressed?' asked the analyst.

'Oh, God no. It was so long ago. I couldn't possibly recall it. I have always been depressed. It has always been there.'

'You mean you can't recall the first day when you felt totally stopped in your tracks, unable to function?'

'No, I can't,' she replied. 'I don't see how that would help, in any event. It's like asking someone the first day they remember coughing, when you already know that the cough is a sign of lung cancer.'

'I don't agree,' said the analyst. 'I respect your decision to take medications and I am sorry that your therapy didn't work. But we get depressed for a reason, or for various reasons, and we must ask what has happened in our life to bring about this kind of pain. Sadly enough, you have been depressed for thirty years, and whatever it was that set this off, whatever events were mentally discarded by you and thrown into your moods, are perhaps lost for ever, and in this way depression is your fate.'

'What an incredibly arrogant thing to say. My depression is endogenous. It is a purely biological event. It's in my genes. My mother was depressed; her mother was depressed. It means nothing – nothing at all. It has nothing to do with thinking or bad experiences or anything of the kind, and I believe your take on medication is destructive. Surely you must acknowledge that there are endogenous depressions?'

'Yes, I do,' said the psychoanalyst. 'I've seen probably three or four biologically-driven depressions in thirty-five years of practice. But I would not call that a significantly high figure, given the hundreds of depressed people whose depressions were reactions to lived experiences that were denied thought.'

'But I know that my depression has nothing to do with me. You would make it my fault and that is morally wrong.'

'Look, my observation is – and you can take it or leave it – that you are clearly an angry woman. You have such high standards that it is impossible for you to allow the fact that your depression may have something to do with you, but your spin seems to be that if it did, then you would be in the wrong.'

'Rubbish,' she said. 'By even allowing this as a possibility, all you do is make me feel worse. You are taking a person suffering from a disease and suggesting that it is their own moral or psychological failure.'

'If that is what I thought, I would say so – but in my view, your paraphrase of my comment rather illustrates my point that you are overly aggressive, and that you silence even the possibility of considering my view.'

'I have to,' she said. 'You have too much authority: I have to defend my view.'

'By closing your mind?'

'My mind is not closed!'

'Well, I accept the correction,' said the analyst. 'You wouldn't be here if your mind was entirely closed.'

'I'm here to tell you that you are wrong, and to protest about your position.'

'No doubt. But if that was *all* you thought, you wouldn't have bothered. When Murk told you about my views, I think it troubled another part of you. I do believe that your mind is not as closed as you think, and indeed I believe – given that you are obviously a talented and successful writer – that there must be a part of you that could give true thought to your condition and—'

'And you think this would help me.'

'Yes,' he said.

'And all those years of therapy?'

'Well, there are as many therapists as there are writers or car mechanics. Some are good enough, and a lot are not so good. I expect you've had bad luck, and I'm sorry about that, but that's life.'

The psychoanalyst was moved by this conversation. Enid Sullivan was a wonderful novelist but in recent years she had become a militant and high-profile advocate for ordinary sufferers of depressive illness. She was a champion of psychotropic intervention, and was violently anti-therapy. Was the analyst to say to her that indeed, too many shrinks were now poorly trained? Only something like twenty percent, he reckoned, knew the basics of psychodynamics. Therapists and even psychoanalysts had, instead, reduced matters to single causes: a mother who did not understand the patient, or a father who put the child in a disassociated state, or an uncle who had been abusive. However severely these facts of a self's life had indeed impacted on the person, it was a sad matter to *reduce* the complexity of the human being in this way. And the biological was now the trumpet of single causation, he thought: the body had become the problem besetting the mind. We were merely derivatives of bio-logic, and the cure was chemical.

What a depressing state of affairs, he thought.

No matter how precise and specific a particular depressive experience might be – a low mark at school, failure in an athletic event, or distress over one's performance at work – we were living in a culture that pushed emotional life (the outcome of mental life) to the side and substituted it with the brain.

Once, he remembered, while attending one of those God-awful 'target point' training seminars, he had found himself in a light-hearted mood, and he had asked the psychotropic team if they believed there was a pill to cure an argument between a husband and a wife. Could a disagreement, for example, over whether one understood the other's sense that the self was not being appreciated, be solved by aspirin? Valium, perhaps? The four panellists looked puzzled and then smiled and said they thought that indeed medication might help, especially Valium. And if the husband called his wife a 'stupid cow', the analyst suggested provocatively, because she had wanted to have children and he could not stand them; and further, if his wife had taken revenge by having an affair with his best friend; and if their four-year-old son was grief-stricken because his father ignored him, because he was replicating his own relation to his father, who would not talk to him; and further, if the wife was suffering recurring nightmares about her own mother's death from cancer two years before? What then? Would the panellists suggest that the whole family went onto Napalmtrek®?

Total silence had followed, but it was not long before the senior member of the panel, Dr Fritz Rich, of the Centre for Neuroscientific Reprogramming at Uxbridge University, argued that all members of the family should have a 'scan' – a PET scan, an MRI plus a full allergy work-up – and that each should then be 'targeted' with specific medications. Dr Rich went on to add that he would have to look carefully at the psychoanalyst's imaginary scenario, but he was sure that if each of the complaints involved in the 'interfertilisation' was isolated and medicated, then the interfertilisation would stop and there would be no further outbreak of difficulty in the family.

Dr Rich had continued talking, other members of the panel had joined in, and it had been clear to the analyst that their view held the day.

As the psychoanalyst waited to see his next depressed patient that afternoon, he did so knowing that people like Myrna Fallbrook and Byron Mourncaster were actually cultural heroes. In facing their depression, they were remaining human. They accepted that suffering was a part of life, but so too was help by a related other. It was strange, he thought to himself, that those who saw themselves as psychologically disturbed were in fact more in touch with themselves, more psychological, than the increasing mass of humanity walking zombie-like down the road of self-elimination.